Underwood, Scotch, and Wry

Underwood, Scotch, and Wry

by
Brian D. Meeks

This is a work of fiction. The characters, events, and story contained within, are created within the fertile imagination of the author. Any resemblance to persons, whether living or dead, or any events, are purely coincidental with the single exception of Nobel physicist Dr. Wolfgang Ketterle who was used with his permission.

No part of this publication may be reproduced in whole or in part, or stored in a retrieval system, or transmitted in any form, by any means electronic, mechanical, printing, photocopying, recording, chiseling in stone, or otherwise, without the written permission from the publisher, except for the inclusion of brief quotations in a review. For information regarding permission contact the publisher.

Copyright© 2015 by Brian D. Meeks All rights reserved.

ISBN: 978-1-9242810-09-4

Chapter One

Monday, a few minutes after noon, he knocked on the imported, mahogany door. The secretary, with her practiced tone of disapproval, had announced his arrival. He walked in and found the President of Beckerston College sharing a cigar with the Dean of Liberal Arts.

He looked at the dean and the president, gave a mocking bow, and said, "I was summoned by your Excellency."

President Jonathan Grosvenor put out his cigar and said, "You're late."

"It is only four minutes after noon."

"Our meeting was at ten."

"I am unfamiliar with this ten thing of which you speak."

"Maybe if you would get up at a reasonable hour once in a while you would be?"

"I'll have you know I arose well before noon to make the trek to your hallowed tower."

Dean Mary Shingle put her cigar down and said, "You live on campus. It is a ten minute walk, and you didn't even bother to shave."

"I didn't realize it was a formal gathering, your grace."

The president took a seat behind his desk. Mary pointed to a chair and said, "The reason we've called you in today is that we're going to need you to take on an additional class."

"I'm far too busy with my novel, and, as I've told you before, I'll not teach the lowly freshmen their English."

She looked at the president. A wry smile settled over top the sour look that was her norm. She said, "Arthur, we wouldn't think of burdening you with English 101. A much more exciting opportunity awaits you. You're being given SMS 301. Dear Mrs. Clayton has, well, let's just say she has become unavailable."

"I'm not familiar with SMS 301, but I know that Mrs. Clayton has run off to Belize with that knobby-kneed buffoon from the history department, Doogie Houser."

"Donald Houserman, and, yes, they've left us in an unfortunate position. We have just over 100 bright-eyed students, many of whom have parents who are very generous and expect the class to be offered. We can hardly disappoint them, can we?"

"I think you'll find that I am more than qualified to disappoint them. One might say there are few things I relish more than crushing the spirits of our..."

"Yes, we are well aware, but this isn't a request."

Arthur, perpetually on the cusp of a hollow threat of quitting, said, "I can't possibly be ready to teach a class about...What is SMS 301?"

President Grosvenor stood and said, "Don't get all worked up, Arthur. It's a new course, cutting-edge really, which was added to the catalog last spring for this fall semester. SMS stands for Social Media Sciences."

"What in God's name is the science of social media and why would you think I could possibly teach this course?"

"You are a writer, and content is king so I'm told. All 104 slots filled up on the first day of registration."

"Content?"

President Grosvenor walked around the desk, a signal that the meeting was coming to a close, and said, "Gladys has a syllabus for you. You'll cover Facebook, Twitter, that sort of thing, but the main focus will be blogging. You do have a computer, don't you?"

Arthur was stunned and didn't hear anything after the word "blogging." He did not personally own a computer and barely tolerated the one that sat in the corner of his office.

"Arthur, if you have any questions, Mary will be happy to give any guidance you might need."

Mary sneered and said, "It would be my pleasure to help any way I can." The "piss off, you arrogant luddite, you're on your own" was implied.

Arthur found his legs and stood. "Blogging?! You want me to teach about blogging? I'd sooner be trampled by a wandering herd of pachyderms or teach sex education to a wondering pack of teenage boys than wade into the great unwashed masses that pour out their failed ambitions on the…" he paused to affix disgust firmly to his face and continued an octave lower, "internet."

"You'll be fine," President Grosvenor said, patting him on the back.

Without looking back, he said, "I know this is your doing, Mary, and you will rue the day that you brought this to my door."

Mary said, "Have a lovely day, Arthur. Your first class is on Wednesday at the Peterson Lecture Hall…8 a.m."

Chapter Two

Edgar's Pit served burgers and fries at a reasonable price, but on Mondays they were half-price. To Arthur, that seemed wholly reasonable, which was why he was a fixture at the end of the bar. More than anything he hated average, fair, or normal. He was always in search of the tail on the bell curve.

"I thought I'd find you here," said Eric.

"Your proclivity for deduction rivals that of the chief resident of 221B Baker Street. Will you be off to the opium dens after lunch?"

"The problem with your sarcasm is that nobody gets your references. I heard you've been assigned to SMS 301."

"They expect me to teach a generation who can't be bothered to use whole words how to blog. The only thing worse than bloggers are the dregs of society that our fine institution of higher learning bilks for their parents' trust fund money," Arthur said as he set his drink down on the manila envelope that Gladys had given him as he was ushered from the President's office.

Eric picked up the syllabus and flipped each page over with no small measure of amusement.

"Have you even used a computer?"

"I have, twice, and I found it to be a mind-numbingly dull experience. I think they're a fad."

"You are far too much of a curmudgeon for your age."

"I'm exactly the right amount of curmudgeon for a man of forty-five," he said, loud enough for the bar manager to hear him.

"You're fifty-three."

"I should think a mathematician of your caliber would be familiar with the concept of rounding."

"How is forty-five a choice for rounding from fifty-three?"

"You should be a blogger. I think high-level math has passed you by."

"What are you going to do?"

"I'm going to drink this fine single malt and finish my fries. Beyond that, I haven't given it much thought."

"I mean about the class."

"I suppose I'll fake it."

"You know why Mary picked you, Dr. Byrne?"

"Because she's a foul woman who hasn't been laid in nigh on twenty years and harbors a deep-seated resentment of my literary achievements."

"You wrote a best seller in 1993, had a small measure of celebrity, and have been trading on it ever since. I think your account is about dry. Have you written anything lately?"

"So I haven't published in the last few years."

"It has been twenty. Twenty years since you've published anything."

Arthur finished his drink, set it on the bar, and, in a combination move, waved his arm to order another drink and dismiss his friend's comment. "What's your point?"

"Mary is trying to get rid of you."

"I have tenure."

"Yes, but the performance clause..."

"I teach three other classes. Doesn't the performance clause say something about 75% of the..."

"It's students; you must fulfill your teaching requirements with regards to 75% of the students who are enrolled in your classes. And how many are in SMS 301?"

"That bitch."

"I don't believe that is a number. Were you rounding again?"

"There are 104."

"And how many are in your other three classes?"

"Less than 312. It's a ridiculous clause. I've never heard of anything like it in academia."

"I think we are the first in the nation to have it, but that isn't the point. You need to make it through the semester, or you're out."

A long silence followed. Eric ordered a burger basket and let Arthur mull things over. A bubbly young woman with a book clutched to her ample bosom eased up next to Arthur and asked, "Dr. Byrne, I was wondering if you would mind signing this?"

The cloud that followed Arthur around always seemed to dissipate when a prospective bad decision hovered nearby. "I'd be happy to. What's your name?"

She smiled. "Clarissa."

"A fine name. Have you read Samuel Richardson?"

"No, what has he written?"

"Among other things, he penned, in 1748 I believe, a novel called, Clarissa: Or the History of a Young Lady," Arthur said as he handed her back the book.

"Do you think they would have it in the library?"

"In fact, I believe they do. It's from a different age, but you may still find it interesting. Are you a student?"

"Yes, Dr. Byrne, I'm a junior, but I just transferred, so this will be my first semester."

"I'm sure you'll find a world of experience that will more than justify the princely tuition you've paid."

"I have a Bequeath Scholarship, but I am sure you are right."

"Really? Then you are a writer as well."

"Not yet, but it's my dream."

"Well, be sure to stop by my office any time if you need a pointer."

"Thanks," she said and floated away.

Arthur's mood was greatly improved.

"So, what are you going to do?"

"I'll not be bullied."

"You'll be out on your ass..."

"I'll be fine. I can always..."

"And you'll no longer have a new crop each year of those adoring wood nymphs you hire as teaching assistants."

The cloud returned. "I'm screwed."

Chapter Three

Arthur, taking a break from his lunch time drinking, snoozed on the couch in his office. A relic from the 70s, the leather was cracked and worn in all the right places and fit him like a twenty-eight-year-old grad student with a history of bad decision making. The knock at the door was not appreciated. "Come in, or, if you have an ounce of decency in you, don't."

"Dr. Byrne," said a woman's voice, which was vastly more acceptable than the alternative.

Without opening his eyes or removing his arm from across his face, Arthur said, "Yes?"

"I'm Wen Hu."

"If you're Wen Hu, then I must be 'What's on Second?' Now state your business and leave me to my slow and steady decline into an abyss of irrelevance."

"What's on second? I don't understand."

Arthur decided to open his eyes on the off chance that his visitor might be attractive. She was. "I'll give you a hint, Bud and Lou. That should be enough for you to look on BoobTube and unravel the mysteries of my reference. If you've got nothing else to do."

"Do you mean YouTube?"

"Use whatever you like. What brings you around during nap time?"

"The other TA's and I would like to know when you planned on getting together."

"There are others?"

"Five of us. I just got the email about you taking over the class this morning."

Arthur got up and took his place behind the desk. He rubbed his temples and said, "Please take a seat, Lou."

"It's Hu."

"I know. Now, presumably since you checked your email, you're one of those people who use computers to waste their time on that internet thing?"

"Yes. It is a class on social media, and, who doesn't use the internet?" she asked. Wen looked at his bare desk and added, "Where is your computer?"

"It is yonder, beneath that stack of Muddy Waters records."

The expression on her face made two things abundantly clear. Wen Hu had heard the rumors about Dr. Byrne but had, until now, assumed they were more urban myth than

13

anything. The realization of truth being exactly as strange as fiction was difficult for her to comprehend. "Yes, it is true, I'm not fond of the computer, which begs the question, why have I been assigned to teach such a dreadful subject?"

"Maybe it's a mistake?"

"Mary Shingle does not make mistakes. It is a superbly calculated move for which I have no reply."

"So, why don't you just knock over your king and be done with it?" she said, growing annoyed with Arthur's self-pity.

"Do you play chess?"

"Yes. Do you know anything about social media?"

"I've heard of tweeter."

"It's Twitter," she said, shaking her head, "Have you read the syllabus?"

"I'm waiting for the movie. I understand it's to be done in 3D and includes cameo appearances by the cast of Glee. It should be an Oscar contender."

"Social media is serious business. It has changed the world."

"I quite doubt that."

"When there were earthquakes in New Zealand, people used Twitter to get word out about missing loved ones. When news breaks, it is usually social media that gets it out first even before the networks. It changes lives, decides elections, and levels the playing field for everyone.

Do you know what the all-time most viewed video is on YouTube?"

"I do not."

"It is by a Korean artist called Psy. A singer that few people outside South Korea had heard of before the video went viral."

"And how many people have watched this Korean singer's video?" Arthur asked, his interest piqued.

"The video has been viewed over one billion times."

Arthur didn't have a clever response or any comment; he just let the number sort of hang there and then said, "It seems you have a real passion for this stuff."

"I do."

"Normally, that is the sort of thing I would find troubling, but with you it is only 89% so."

"Was that a compliment?"

"It was not. It was a carefully considered analysis. I don't do compliments, nor do I eat peas or tolerate fruit in Jello."

"Fruit in Jello?"

"It is an abomination, and people who wed two wonderful things into such an unholy union should be killed."

"You're quite a mess, aren't you?"

"Yes. Your point?"

Wen stood up, removed the Muddy Waters records, and opened the computer box. "Where do you want it?"

"Any response that I might choose, I fear has been done, so I'll just let that one pass."

Five minutes later Wen had his computer up and running. Thirty minutes after that, Arthur had learned the terms "browser" and "URL" and found it too taxing to go on. He suggested they go for a drink. She suggested, with quite a bit more force, that they go buy him a smart phone.

"But if I have one of those cellular phone devices, won't people be able to call me? Isn't it really just a new fangled leash on which those who annoy most may tug whenever they fancy?"

"Yes. I'll make sure they have the shock collar app installed before you leave the store," she said with a smile that didn't give any hint as to whether she was kidding.

"It can't really shock me, can it?"

"This is going to be an interesting semester."

Chapter Four

The late afternoon sun seemed to take some of the edge off Wen Hu as Arthur led her to his parking spot. She hadn't stopped talking since leaving his office. He wasn't listening much, but the gist seemed to be that she took her TA job seriously and wasn't going to let his need for a crash computer course stop them from enriching the minds of any who took the class. "I believe that if one attends class and pays attention, then they will have every opportunity to earn a passing grade."

"Would you describe yourself as an easy or hard grader?" Arthur asked, figuring that her response might be long enough that he could zone out and have a pleasant, little virtual nap.

"Hard. You?"

Damn, he thought, not at all prepared for a serious discussion. He said, "I've been described as tough but fair in my real classes, but for SMS 301 I thought I'd employ one of those indecipherable check, check plus, check minus systems that so many of my colleagues use to allow them to give A's to students they really like and F's to students who have the temerity to think for themselves."

"I hate those systems. Why do they do that?"

"Because, in most cases, they lack the reasoning and math skills of a mildly retarded newt."

"You can't say that."

"I'm not always politically incorrect, but when I am, I prefer to pick on a group with very little lobbying muscle. Do you have strong feelings about the family Salamandridae?"

"I thought you were talking about the politician."

"I wasn't."

"Well then, I suppose it is okay, just don't pick on pandas."

"I would never."

"Is that your car?"

"It's a classic 1957 Triumph TR3, and I'll not tolerate any disparaging remarks about her. She is the love of my life."

"She's cute in a middle-life crisis sort of way."

"If I had a child and had to choose, well, there would be one more orphan."

Wen Hu climbed into the tiny sports car. Arthur pulled a pair of pretentious driving gloves from his pocket, placed the key into the ignition, and paused to give the moment the reverence it deserved, before twisting his wrist. The engine roared in an understated British sort of way. He said, "Put your seat belt on, Lou." The car pulled away with a satisfying roar.

"It's Hu."

"What's on second? I don't know who's on first."

"That's getting old fast."

"Until you get the joke, I'm going to stay with it."

Wen Hu whipped out her iPhone, and her thumbs began to pound on the screen. Arthur barely had time to ponder what she might be up to when he heard the familiar routine. He was both impressed and a little horrified at how quickly she found it. Wen laughed a little.

Wen put her phone away and said, "We're here."

"I see that," said Arthur in a voice that was decidedly unexcited.

"The Apple store doesn't have curb service; we'll need to go in."

"I'm saying a prayer."

"What for?"

"I'm saying a little something lamenting the loss of the life I've so enjoyed. I shall never again be able to unleash a torrent of derision at Eric when he giggles like a schoolgirl at each new Apple announcement. It's really vulgar."

"What?"

"His fanboydom."

"You know the term 'fanboy'?"

"Eric explained it to me between Applegasms the night before the iPhone 4S came out. He was standing on that very spot, there," Arthur said, pointing towards the sidewalk outside the Apple store.

"Who is Eric?"

"He is one of a very small list of people I can tolerate for extended periods of time."

"How many lists do you suppose you're on?"

Arthur undid his seatbelt and got out of the car. The smirk on Wen's face was noted and filed away for a future rebuttal.

Wen held the door for Arthur who paused and then was thrust into the 21st century by his feisty new TA's double-hand push to the back. If Arthur were to guess, she had to put all hundred pounds of her into the shove.

A woman with an air of suburbia housewife, in a blue "genius" shirt, smiled as if she weren't peddling wares that were surely the first sign of the apocalypse, and asked, "How may I help you, today?"

Arthur affixed his best nonchalant expression, which did an admirable job of hiding his fear of looking stupid. Answering in a similarly calm fashion was more than he could muster. He focused on the woman's name tag, which read Allison.

Wen said, "Professor Byrne needs a new phone."

Allison said, "What type of phone are you looking to upgrade from?"

Wen said, "His phone is probably a little older than he would care to admit. Why don't we just see what you have?"

"Well, as you know, the iPhone 5s is out and is very exciting. The apps are wonderful. Would you like to see one?"

Arthur didn't know what an app was, but it was the sort of question he could answer without fear of messing up. He said, "Yes, please."

For the next ten minutes, Allison Suburbia talked about features, her voice rising more than an octave at the really important parts. He wondered if she had a teen-age daughter going through her "OMG" shouting phase. His writer's mind kept him entertained as she droned on about things beyond his ability to comprehend or appreciate. Allison Suburbia was easily encouraged with gentle nods of fauxstanding, he thought. He made a mental note to write "fauxstanding" down later. Making up words made Arthur happy.

Arthur said yes to a question he hadn't heard, which led to a typing of and adding up prices that almost caused him to black out. Somehow, Wen had his credit card and was explaining iTunes. Arthur had heard of iTunes, and because of his love of music, it seemed far less objection-able than anything else said. He decided to pay attention.

Wen explained downloading, and Arthur had the presence of mind to make a suggestion. A moment later he had purchased "Messin' with the Man." Arthur hit play and said, "Originally done by Junior Wells. This was released on the Chess label in 1961."

Allison said, "I don't know much about music, but I like how it sounds. It's good."

Arthur smiled, "Louis Armstrong once said, 'If it sounds good, it is good.'"

Allison said, "Well, you can find almost any song imaginable on iTunes, and, of course, there are lots of fun apps."

Wen got excited and asked if she could borrow Arthur's new phone. He shrugged and handed it to her. When she handed it back, it had another app on it. She said, "This is a game I just bought for you - well, you bought it, but I think you'll like it."

Arthur looked at her and said, "So, are we done spending my money?"

"You've got a case, a plan, and a phone. We're done for now."

Arthur thanked Allison, and he and Wen Hu left. While he drove Wen back to campus, she programmed in her phone number and downloaded the Twitter app, explaining that she would help him set up all the important stuff tomorrow.

When Arthur got home, he set his new phone down next to the rotary phone on the kitchen counter. He opened the refrigerator as he often did only to curse his meager selection of choices. There were bananas and cheese. He grabbed a banana and picked up the rotary phone and dialed China House but hung up before they answered.

He wanted to curl up and sulk, but Arthur summoned all his strength. Using his new iPhone 5s, he pushed the little phone icon and dialed the number for China House again. There were few things that a massive helping of shrimp lo mein couldn't cure.

Chapter Five

As a hobby, waxing nostalgic was nearer to poison than drug. Arthur slid the vinyl from its sleeve and carefully placed the needle down. It was the second copy of Who's Next he had owned. In mint condition like all of his albums, Roger Daltrey, Pete Townshend, Keith Moon, and John Entwistle sounded as good as they had the first time he heard them in 1971.

The dumplings were fine, and the lo mein would keep until tomorrow, but the twelve-year old Glen Moray was like a warm, familiar, blanket. Arthur pushed aside the day's events, closed his eyes, and tiptoed back to the tiny apartment in the village on the west side of Lower Manhattan. The record was playing there, too. Between songs, Arthur returned to the present.

Less than six feet away on a writing desk sat his lonely typewriter, dusty and without a voice. A crisp stack of paper was at the ready and, with the exception of the top sheet, would be glad to accept a tale. Arthur didn't have a story to tell.

Students, en route to bars, laughed with the Joie de vivre that comes with a life yet lived. Arthur watched from his porch. A small black cat appeared on the railing and said, "Meow."

"I've nothing for you. 'Get thee back into the tempest and the Night's Plutonian Shore.'"

Quoth the kitty, "Meow."

"I can see that was lost on you, little furry one. Such is life," Arthur said. He stood and went back inside. The final song neared the end, and he returned the needle to its carriage. His own ominous bird of yore sat stately upon his kitchen counter. He dialed one of the few numbers he knew and waited.

"Hello, this is Eric."

"Eric, what are you up to?"

"Where are you calling from?"

"I've been pulled kicking and screaming into a new century."

"Do you mean this century or the last?"

"I am the less than proud owner of an iPhone 5s."

"Good for you. You coming down to the bar?"

"I might. I just wanted to make sure this thing worked."

25

"See you later," Eric said. The background noise of a new semester-in-wait ended.

Arthur did like the look of the phone but not so much that he wanted to waste any more time goofing around with it. The Tiffany lamp cast an easy light on his favorite chair. The book that waited wasn't what he needed. Arthur went back to his bedroom and pulled Elmore Leonard's Djibouti off the shelf. He had bought it a couple of years ago but not gotten around to giving it a look. Arthur used to read E.L. all the time back in the day.

The pages were just as brilliant as he knew they would be. He drank in the dialog. The hours were pleasant, and the drink did its job.

He had been dreaming when the horrible sound of an alarm shook him awake. The book, still on his lap, fell to the floor. It was morning. Arthur was confused. The sound didn't stop, so he got up and found that his phone was making all the racket. "Hello?"

"It's Wen. Good morning, Dr. Byrne."

"First of all, why would I possibly want to be up before noon on my last day to sleep in, and, secondly, there has never been such a thing as a good morning."

"I'll bring you a coffee to the meeting."

"What meeting?"

"I took the liberty of scheduling a meeting with the rest of the TAs. I was sure you'd want to meet everyone before tomorrow."

"What time is it?"

"It is 7:30. I've already been jogging."

"What the hell is wrong with you, Lou?"

"Nothing. I'm young."

"I'm going back to bed," he said and hung up.

The doorbell rang. Arthur's head was throbbing more than most days, and he was prepared to give the Mormons a piece of his mind. He swung open the door to find his annoyingly eager TA standing before him. "Lou, you've got the tenacity of one of those really annoying little dogs that people tend to tire of and leave at kill shelters."

She thrust her hand forward and said, "Double mocha latte."

"Thanks, come in. I'll take a shower and then we can drop you at the shelter. Help yourself to either a piece of cheese or a banana."

One hour and seven minutes later Arthur stood before a crowd of young people all with the same eager look that Wen flaunted at every turn. "I suppose we should begin with introductions as we are going to be suffering through this semester together unless I decide to take the coward's way out...which is likely. I'm Dr. Byrne, and I teach literature. I do not, as Lou can attest..."

A smartly dressed man, probably mid-twenties, said, "Who's Lou? Is he dreamy?"

"Wen can explain how I've come to call her Lou later, but for now let's just assume our brief time together will be unpleasant. That being said, it is probably best not to form any attachments with ritualistic name learning, so Kurt, to answer your question, Lou is not your type, I'd wager."

The smartly dressed man said, "Did you call me Kurt because of Glee?"

"Was that offensive?" Arthur said, not really caring.

"Now he is dreamy...so, no, I'll take it. Are you a 'gleek', Dr. Byrne?"

"I don't think I rise to the level of gleek per se, but I've taken in an episode or two."

"You know, I am totally a gleek. I simul-tweet every episode and host a chat afterwards."

"Moving on. Obviously, you're Lawrence."

"Why can't I be Barack?"

"Because I am going to need you to 'act' like a social media professional, not the President. If you get Oprah's endorsement, we can change your nickname."

A nervous redhead averted her eyes.

"You'll be..."

"Susan?"

"Definitely not...okay, you can be Susan, only because I don't care for Pippy and I think Wendy's could do a better job with their fries."

The red haired girl looked relieved.

Arthur paused, partly for effect and partly to survey the young man. His bushy eyebrows and receding hairline didn't really work for his age. The skate punk t-shirt seemed to make sense and went well with his teenaged goth angst frame, but Arthur couldn't get past wanting him to have a bushy mustache to go with the eyebrows. He said, "And you, you shall be Rudyard."

He looked at Arthur and said, "What sort of name is Rudyard?"

"I thought you might be interesting, like the extraordinary writing of Rudyard Kipling. You have his eyebrows, but, alas, it seems I've misjudged. You shall be A."

"A what?"

"Just the letter A. If you are good, I might be willing to give you a consonant or two to go with it."

Kurt said, "Dr. B, what is your background in social media? I googled you, and I didn't find anything. Well, except that you wrote a book."

"You have uncovered my terrible secret. I'm literate and prefer books. I've been given this horrible assignment as punishment for living a life that suits me."

"So, how are you going to teach a class about..."

"That is a reasonable question, but the more important question is how is it going to reflect on you, my bright-eyed Glee enthusiast."

"Okay, how is it going to reflect on us?"

"Though I am likely to be a horrific teacher of social media, I am able to craft superb letters of recommendation that will make a prospective employer weep. So, though the next few months will be a burden, and I will do as little as possible to pull my weight, if we survive, I will make it right for you all with the power of my pen."

Lawrence said, "Cool."

Susan didn't look sure, but Kurt seemed happy with the answer. A. had stopped listening and was furiously texting. Arthur was pleased with himself and declared the meeting adjourned.

Chapter Six

Arthur gave a lengthy explanation of how much he didn't wish to be disturbed. His secretary had heard it before but rarely with such numerous references to medieval torture devices. He locked his door and turned off the lights she turned on each morning.

Arthur moved the mouse, the computer came to life, and he clicked on the browser icon. He knew two things about computers, and he had just exhausted 50 percent of his knowledge with his first click. He went to the URL, his second bit of computer understanding, and typed www.google.com.

The page was clean and uncluttered, which provided no small measure of comfort. Arthur stared at it. He took in all the white space and let it wash over him. Tomorrow, he was to pass himself off as an expert in something that every single student had been using since before puberty.

There wouldn't be one among them who saw this screen and had their stomach knot with worry about what to do next.

Arthur pulled a yellow pad from his desk and ground a brand new Dixon Ticonderoga No. 2 into a fine point. He wrote, Twitter, Facebook, and LinkedIn. His fingers tapped, How do I...He stopped as a little window started trying to guess what he wanted to do. He added the word register, and Google, in bold, suggested "to vote, a business name, my Kindle."

I don't have a Kindle, but it seems to know I like books, Arthur thought. Arthur also thought of a Connecticut Yankee in King Arthur's Court. He was the rube being amazed by the strange man from the future. He didn't like feeling like a dullard.

For a Twitter account? The little, blue button with the magnifying glass was the only button, so he clicked on it. His first search returned 88,600,000 results, a number that was staggering except in politics. The first result he read aloud was "Twitter/Create an Account." His hand hovered over the mouse and was brought back.

He wrote on the yellow pad, How do I register for a Twitter account?

Arthur typed, How do I keep from looking stupid in class? The first few results of the 126,000,000 available seemed unhelpful, but it was obvious one could ask Google anything. That was comforting. Why do I feel so tired?

he thought. He went back to his first search and clicked on the link to Twitter.

The first question was simple, his full name, but then it got complicated. Twitter wanted to know his email address. Arthur didn't know his email address. His secretary did, but she would give him a disapproving look if he asked. It seemed Arthur had no recourse. He would take a nap.

The nap wasn't restful.

Arthur went to Edgar's Pit and ordered a full-price burger basket, which still seemed to be underpriced. Most days he would have sat at the bar but today he took a booth in the back. Eric found him anyway.

"Let's see it."

Arthur took out his phone and laid it on the table. Eric nodded and said, "You made a good choice." Eric picked it up and fiddled with it for a minute. "What's your iTunes password?"

Arthur told him and asked, "What are you doing?"

Eric didn't answer. He chuckled to himself and took a picture. "Okay, I put in your email address and phone number. Check this out. Here, take your phone."

Arthur took the phone back and set it on the table.

"No, hold it up."

He slumped his shoulders and said, "You're becoming tedious."

Eric bumped his phone against Arthur's and said, "There, now you have all my important information, and I have yours. Pretty cool, huh?"

"What do you mean important information?"

"We just exchanged phone numbers and email addresses. Go to your address book."

Arthur looked at the screen blankly.

"It's the green one in the bottom corner with the phone on it. Okay, now choose the little guy at the bottom. That is your contact book. Address book for old people like you."

"It pains me to say it, but that was a nice piece of technology witchcraft."

"If anyone else has the Bump app, you can just hit the phones together."

The burger basket arrived. Eric ordered one, too. A moment later Wen rushed in and yelped, "I found you!"

Arthur popped a fry in his mouth and said, "Obviously the cloaking app isn't working."

"I went to your office, but your secretary said you weren't there. I've been to the library, your house, and even the grocery store."

Eric laughed.

"What's so funny?"

"You've never seen his refrigerator."

"Hi, I'm Wen Hu."

"Hello, Wen, I'm Eric. Why are you chasing our grumpy, old friend here?"

"I'm one of his TAs, and we need to get ready for class tomorrow."

"It is nice to meet you."

"It's nice to meet one of Professor Byrne's friends."

Eric smiled, "Well, it may be a while before you find another one. We're a rare species."

Arthur said, "I had plenty of friends, but they all died."

Wen looked shocked and asked, "All of them?"

"Yes, Mark died to a woman in Arizona who bore him three burdens. Jerry died to a dreadful hair stylist in Las Vegas with spectacular...well, you get the idea."

Wen rolled her eyes and asked, "Do you take anything seriously?"

"I take many things seriously. Rudyard Kipling, Harper Lee, Oscar Wilde, and Elmore Leonard are all held in the highest regard. I am dead serious when I discuss the many reasons that Ernest Hemingway's greatest contribution to literature was his generous decision to take his own life. I will not be sucked into a discussion of politics by people who prefer emotion to reason. The designated hitter is an abomination, and the day pitchers and catchers report is the start of the new year despite what those ill-informed calendar makers might try to tell you."

"I didn't understand most of that. I'm glad, though. Now, do you know your email address?"

"Yes, I do. Check the Bump app. It's in there."

"You have Bump," she sounded shocked as she tapped her phone against his.

Arthur said, "I like to stay on the cutting edge of technology."

The waitress returned and Wen slid in next to Eric. She ordered a burger basket, too, and went to work on the phone.

Chapter Seven

Mary raised her glass and said, "Here is to the start of a wonderful, new semester."

Dr. Weaverson said, "A clean slate of young minds is always an exciting thing and worthy of a toast."

"To a clean slate."

The mood was jovial, and the conversation lighthearted. When the dinner plates had been cleared and the tiramisu had been set before her guests, Mary said, "I hope you have all enjoyed yourselves, but, truth be told, I had an ulterior motive in inviting you here this evening."

Mr. Evans said, "How ominous and delightful. After such a delicious meal, I am more than willing to do your bidding."

"Thank you Mr. Evans. As you all know, well, all of you except our newest colleague," Mary said with a smile towards Dr. Emily Bird. She continued, "We have a faculty member who is a constant source of embarrassment for both our fine college and all who devote their lives to making this the best institution of higher learning possible. He mocks all that we hold dear."

Dr. Weaverson and Mr. Evans nodded with understanding. Emily Bird asked, "Who is this notorious professor?"

"Arthur Byrne."

"The writer?"

"The skirt-chasing drunk is a more apt moniker. As far as I know, he hasn't written anything in over a decade."

Mr. Evans asked, "How can we help, Mary?"

"I'm not asking for you to do anything unseemly. Just attend his class tomorrow and write a brief summary of his performance."

"Is that all?" he asked then added, "You didn't need to wine and dine me for that, but I'm glad you did."

"To be honest, I wouldn't be surprised if he didn't bother to get out of bed."

* * *

8 am, Peterson Lecture Hall

Dr. Weaverson, sitting between Mr. Evans and Dr. Bird, said, "By my watch it is time for class to begin. It figures."

Mr. Evans jotted a note.

A nervous-looking woman peered from behind the curtain.

Dr. Weaverson asked, "So, tell me, Emily, how are you settling into our little community?"

"It's lovely. I especially like the book shop on Main, and the student union is impressive for a school of this size."

Mr. Evans said, "Yes, we are quite proud of it. I chaired the fundraising committee that got that ball rolling."

"Mr. Evans did yeoman's work in rounding up donors."

The din of chatter calmed as a woman approached the lectern. "Hello, my name is Wen Hu, and I'm one of the TAs for this semester. Dr. Byrne will be here shortly. Until then, why don't I introduce the others?"

Five minutes passed. Wen was running out of song and dance. She kept looking to stage left, which did little to persuade the class that Dr. Byrne was actually on his way. At ten minutes past eight, she returned to the microphone and said, "I think we should just..."

A booming voice from the middle of the auditorium said, "Don't be so hasty."

Wen looked at the crowd and said with some relief, "Dr. Byrne," and started to clap. Nobody knew what was going on, but a few students clapped, too.

Arthur removed his hoodie and stood up. "We live in a new era," he said as he walked to the aisle. "When Guttenberg invented his printing press, it brought the written

39

word to the masses. No longer were books the domain of the privileged."

Heads turned, and people craned their necks to see Arthur speak. He continued, "Media has, for centuries, been controlled by a few. The gatekeepers, if you will, deciding what is news and what is unworthy. They wrote the reviews, told us which plays to see, and warned us when Mother Nature was on the cusp of a hissy fit." Arthur didn't head for the stage but walked up and down the aisles with all the showmanship of P.T. Barnum.

A phone rang, and a nervous voice said, "Sorry, sir, I thought it was off."

"What would Alexander Graham Bell have thought were he with us today? To see his idea flourish to become not only an integral part of our lives but almost an extension of our bodies. What is your name, young man?" he asked, making his way towards the student.

"David, sir."

Arthur chuckled, "You may call me Arthur. 'Sir' seems far too formal. Who was calling you, David?"

There was a long silence and he said, "My mother." A few aw's could be heard but mostly laughter.

"Everyone loves a call from mom."

Another voice yelled, "You've never met my mom." There was more laughter.

"I stand corrected. And that is why we are here because social media has the ability to wrest the power of truth from the few and give it to the world. You are the media of the future, you are the keepers of what will be consumed, you, my bright eyed lads and lassies," he said, donning a Scottish accent, "shall shepherd in the next evolution of society."

Someone else yelled, "Amen." Another round of laughter erupted.

Arthur climbed to the stage, walked the length, and walked back again. "I see we have several distinguished faculty members with us today. No doubt concerned about the heresy I might be preaching for we are part of the ruling class. We tell you what to think, but what if... we simply taught you to think for yourselves? What if we showed you how to make your college days more than beer and football? What if we explored Facebook and Twitter and dug beneath the surface?" Arthur preached and took a moment to let a silence shroud the room. With a softer voice he asked, "How many of you are on Facebook?"

Almost everyone shot a hand in the air.

"How many of you are on Twitter?"

Over half the hands came down.

"How many of you know exactly what you are going to do with the rest of your lives?"

All but a few of the most optimistic hands disappeared.

Arthur continued to pace. He brought his voice back up to theatrical level and said, "It looks like there are 80

41

young minds who managed to get out of bed at this unholy hour, which means that about 20 percent of this
class didn't. I applaud you all. For your first assignment
and mine, we...and I mean WE are all going to create new
Twitter accounts. I know there are some of you who probably have put in a fair amount of effort and don't want
to start anew, but today we begin a journey together so
we all start from scratch. If you need to, go get a new
Gmail account. I got mine last night. My twitter handle is @ExtraAmbivalent. All you need to do, to get the
first twenty points of this class is set up an account, write
a clever bio, and follow me. Now, there are likely those
among you who are ambitious. If you want to earn the
easiest extra credit ever just follow your fellow classmates'
new accounts. Oh, and one more thing, the twenty points
is only good for the next twenty-four hours...make that
twenty-eight...ish. My team of crack TAs will go through
and count how many of your fellow classmates you've followed."

Spontaneous chatter rose from the crowd. Wen stood,
but Arthur gave her an "it's okay" look and she sat back
down. He let the murmur continue as he made his way to
the front of the stage.

Arthur stopped and reached into his pocket. He took
out his phone and gave a quick glance.

A smile crept across Arthur's face. "Is there a Josephine
here today?"

A woman with long, chocolate-brown hair raised her hand. She was sitting in the first row and smiling. She held her phone in hand.

"Josephine, can you guess why I have called you out today?"

"Because I've just earned twenty points?"

"Yes, it is! In the brief time I was blathering on about how the class works, Josephine set up an account and followed me. Social media is that easy. Any questions?"

"Why is social media important?"

"That is really two questions: Why is it important on a macro scale? The more interesting question is why is it important to each of you? We will study the former over the rest of the semester, but the latter is easy."

Mr. Evans scrawled notes while Dr. Weaverson sat with arms crossed, shaking his head at every opportunity. Emily seemed to be playing with her phone and not really paying attention.

"Most of you have indicated that you're unsure what the future holds, but whether you leave here and practice law, become a rocket scientist, or find yourself as a low-level manager in a cubicle of death, knowing how the world works and being able to reach into the depths of the dreck that fills up the worldwide web and retrieve something of value or, better yet, demonstrate that you have peoples' ear, will help you to get beyond the mediocrity of your fellow classmates and truly grab that brass ring."

A hand went up.

"Yes?"

"I've never understood why one is grabbing a brass ring and not gold or something like that?"

"A bit off topic, but in the days of your grandparents, before the Xbox, people went on dates to places like Coney Island. There one would find a merry-go-round and if one leaned really far out, a brass ring could be grabbed, and later redeemed for prizes, but it took courage. Basically, it means sticking your neck out to try to impress the girl you just blew your entire paycheck on. Okay, that isn't exactly what it means, but you get my point. Without risk there is no reward despite what you may have learned from watching reality TV. I mean, do you really want your success to come from being named Snooki?"

"Snooki rocks," came a voice from the back.

Arthur grinned and looked at Wen who was now sitting in the front row. He said, "Please find that misguided youth, explain the error of his ways, and deduct two points from his grade."

Everyone laughed.

"I'm just kidding...as far as that student knows...The point I'm trying to make is that this semester we are all going to build something. We are going to use the tools that the evolution of our society has given us and craft something more valuable than the sheep skin you'll frame after graduation. We will be building a giant microphone so that each of us may be heard."

Another hand went up.

"Yes, the young man with the Cubs hat."

"Can you explain how the grading will be done?"

"Each student will be judged harshly, and those found to be worthy will receive a mark commensurate with their performance."

All but a few of the faces were blank; a few looked frightened.

"It will be points, standard 90 percent, 80 percent, et cetera...It is explained in the syllabus that my team of TAs will hand out."

He checked his phone and said, "It seems a young woman named Emily has also gotten a jump on her homework. Emily, would you mind standing up?"

She stood and said, "I'm not sure that "young" is appropriate. I'm not really a student, but I just might have to audit your class."

"As long as there is a seat, all are welcome. In three months we will change how you think about the world and, more importantly, how the world sees you. With that, I'll see you all Friday morning. TAs unleash the syllabi."

Arthur walked off stage right. Every student stood and cheered.

Dr. Weaverson said, "What a dreadful display."

Mr. Evans stopped writing long enough to say, "It was shameful. He has no regard for proper decorum."

Emily said, "I liked it."

They both gave her a weak smile.

Arthur didn't return to his office after his exit and there were three hours to kill before his next class. He wanted a drink. The cheers were intoxicating, but their echoes took him back to the last time he had lectured in front of so many.

The air had seemed too heavy to breathe. Four hundred students and faculty showing their appreciation as he walked on stage. For three days he had fussed over his speech only to have it all vanish like a morning mist the moment he got to the microphone.

She wore a maroon silk top and sat in the front row. Her angelic eyes and unwavering support had kept him at the typewriter day after day until finally he had written "The End." She found the publisher, too. He found new words and said them to her, and it didn't matter if everyone else listened in as he did.

It had been the happiest time of his life. It hadn't lasted. The adoration became a habit he fed in ways she couldn't live with. When it was gone, he turned to drink.

Last he knew, she had given up on life and gotten married...happily.

The arboretum was nice. Arthur contented himself watching squirrels. They seemed to be in fine spirits.

Chapter Eight

"Scotch, neat," Arthur said as he walked in the door.

Donna, the bartender, said, "You want me to bring it over to your group?"

"I wasn't aware I had a group."

"There is a pack of TAs in the corner that made me promise to send you their way as soon as you arrived."

"How did they know I would be arriving?"

"Because you're a creature of habit."

"I really am, and one of my favorites is drinking alone."

A voice carried across the bar and likely all the way to the state border," Dr. Byrne, we're over here."

"Is there a small, enthusiastic Asian woman hailing me?"

"There is," said Donna, setting the drink on the bar.

"If you see this run dry..."

"Got it."

Arthur made his way to the two tables that had been pushed together. There were pitchers of beer, a couple of laptops, an iPad, and two baskets of popcorn.

Wen could barely contain herself. "Dr. Byrne, you were awesome today!"

Kurt said, "You really were."

Arthur took a seat and looked at Kurt, mostly because he hoped the blinding smile on Wen would fade, and asked, "On a scale of one to Gaga, how would you rate it?"

"A solid eight, but I'm a tough grader."

"Good, that's what I want. Take a gold star out of petty cash, Kurt."

Wen said, "You must have stayed up all night writing that speech."

"No, I did exactly as I told you I would. I faked it."

The smooth baritone voice of Lawrence said, "You had me convinced you knew what you were talking about."

"Thanks, but that was the entire bag of tricks. We've still got a few classes left. Any ideas?"

Susan raised her hand.

"You're a TA now, Susan, you don't need to raise your hand."

"Sorry. Maybe the next lecture should be about some of the finer points of Twitter?"

A was texting away and said, "The students seemed pretty fired up to start their accounts. It seems like a good plan."

Susan blushed a little.

Arthur finished his scotch and raised the glass to the heavens. A voice from afar said, "I'm on it."

Arthur asked, "So, what are the finer points of Twitter?"

Wen said, "Let's brainstorm." She began banging on her laptop.

"How about we start with some brain light raining," Arthur suggested.

Wen wrinkled her nose and said, "We should talk about hashtags."

"What's a hashtag?"

Kurt said, "It is a way to group tweets."

Arthur's blank expression spoke volumes.

Kurt continued, "If you're watching Glee alone at home and do a search with a octothorpe - that's what we call a hashtag - you'll find all the tweets relating to the show."

"Interesting. So if I wanted to find people who like Harper Lee, I would just put her name after a pound sign?" Arthur asked.

Wen said, "Let me try." A moment later she spun around her computer. "See, there are mostly quotes from To Kill a Mockingbird, but I'm sure those people all like her writing."

Lawrence said, "We should probably discuss junk followers, too."

Arthur asked, "What's a junk follower?"

"Someone that just wants you to follow them back."

"What's wrong with following people back?"

"Nothing, but the spammers don't really care what you are tweeting or talking about. They just want you to click on their links and promote their crap."

"Those bastards!"

"You joke, but if one is serious about building a following, they just clutter up things."

"Did you get that Wen?"

"Oh, yes."

"Good, now why would someone tweet in the first place?"

A. said, "You wrote a book, right?"

"An earlier version of me did, yes."

"How did you get sales?"

"They trickled in, but I have no idea from where."

"But you got royalties, right?"

"Yes."

"Okay, imagine that people who like your book followed you on Twitter."

"I can do that."

"Now, let's say you have 10,000 fans who follow and you're about to release a new book."

"Unlikely, but I'm with you."

"You could tell them the launch date; you could interact with readers, thus making them more loyal; or you could find new readers by tweeting interesting stuff about your life."

"So, a well-built twitter following, without junk followers, is a marketing tool?"

Lawrence broke in, "Yes, but you need to avoid being marketing all the time. People hate that."

Arthur nodded, "I would hate that."

Wen asked, "How do all of you feel about 'Pls RT'?"

Everyone but Arthur seemed to dislike the concept. He remained nonplussed. Wen asked, "Do you know what I mean, Dr. Byrne?"

"I have no idea."

Lawrence said, "It is when people beg you to retweet their tweet."

"Why would anyone retweet something that has already been said once?"

Wen said, "You have to understand that the only people who see your tweets are the ones who follow you."

"I can see that."

"So, let's say you tweet something about a new book. One of your 10,000 followers takes that tweet and retweets it to their 100 followers because they adore your writing, and it extends your reach."

A. said, "Retweets also show people you are not just a one-way street."

"Okay, A., you've lost me."

A. continued, "People are more likely to help you with your goals if you help them with theirs."

"Is everyone selling something?"

Lawrence said, "No, a lot of people just like hanging out but maybe they have a friend who just put up a new blog post, and they want to help him promote it. If you help, they will appreciate it."

Wen said, "Which brings up a good point..."

"I'm not sure how many more good points I can digest."

"...you want to be careful about blindly tweeting something with a link, especially blog posts, because it might be something you don't want to endorse."

"A retweet equals an endorsement?"

A. said, "Do you want to retweet an article about a Nazi who kicks babies and eats unicorns?"

"I am definitely con Nazis, pro unicorns, and indifferent towards baby kicking...are they kicking for distance or accuracy?"

"Distance."

"Is that measured in yards or with the crazy metric system?"

Donna brought over the fresh scotch and said, "Sorry, it got busy, and I'm short-handed."

53

"Well, in the interest of making your life easier, why don't I order another now and you get it to me whenever it suits you."

"You're a doll."

"You mind tweeting that…gorgeous?"

Donna walked away with a little extra swing in her hips. Arthur watched and it was apparent that the impromptu meeting had been adjourned. He had lost interest in social media.

Chapter Nine

Eric walked over to Arthur and his TAs, beer in hand, and asked to nobody in particular, "How did it go today?"

Wen said, "He was fantastic." Everyone but Arthur agreed.

Arthur stood and said, "I'm going to go hang out and have grown-up time. Toodles."

Eric said, "Don't listen to him, he isn't always this gruff...usually it is much worse."

Arthur made a noise that could easily be described as guttural contempt and wandered off. The bar was, among other things, a wonderful collection of alcoves and nooks with a fair number of crannies thrown in for good measure. If one wanted to revel with the masses, that was fine, but a somewhat quiet conversation could be had as well.

The booth, Arthur's favorite, was far enough away from the main bar that few ventured past. The waitresses always knew where he was, and that was what mattered. Eric joined his friend, ordered a pitcher, and asked, "So what's the real scoop? What did you talk about?"

"I mostly just made it up as I went along. Told everyone to set up a Twitter account and, if they didn't, they would be judged harshly before God Almighty."

"No, you didn't."

"Okay, I may not have mentioned any religious deity, but it was implied."

"And did you put the fear of God into your students?"

"They cheered when I left the stage mostly because class was going to end early."

A waitress brought a pitcher and an extra glass. She left and a woman in a nice blouse and skirt took her place by the table and said, "I'm not sure that was why they were cheering."

Eric said, "Hello."

"Hi, I'm Emily. I sat in on the class. I must say, your friend here put on quite the show."

Arthur looked at her and couldn't think of anything snarky to say, so he went with, "Thanks. Would you like to join us?"

"Sure."

She slid into the booth next to Eric, and he said, "You're a bit more...mature, than most of our students."

"I'm a new associate professor in the French department. Today was my first day of class."

Arthur said, "Welcome to our fine institution of higher learning, well, institution at least."

"I'm pleased to be here."

The next half hour was filled with the rudimentary question and answer session that one finds when meeting new people. Arthur didn't like new people, but Eric seemed quite enchanted with Emily. Eric impressed easily. Arthur did have to admit she was nice looking.

He made every effort to keep his "Arthurness" to a minimum for Eric's sake. When it seemed that a reasonable amount of politeness had been exchanged, Arthur excused himself and snuck out the back door to go home.

The walk was nice. One of the fraternities was grilling something that smelled terrific. Arthur found himself trying to accurately describe the aroma in his mind as he used to do when he was writing. He liked to include passing references for each of the five senses in his works. It was a small detail and likely unappreciated by most, but Arthur wasn't writing for most people; he was writing for one.

The walk up to his porch was interrupted by a tiny "Meow."

"I see we meet again small, furry one."

The black kitten rubbed against his leg and purred.

"Didn't we already discuss that I have nothing for you?"

The next meow was considerably sadder. The purring stopped. The cat curled up on the first step and laid its head on its paws.

Arthur looked at the little beast, swore, and turned around to head to the store a few blocks down. He was hungry anyway.

He bought a large Coke, two sandwiches, and two cans of cat food. When he got back to the house, the little cat was still on the step. He opened a can of cat food and said, "Okay, you've worn me down. Here, you can start on this. I'll get you some water, but don't think it means we're friends."

The cat buried his face in the can of food. It was gone before Arthur returned with a small dish of water. There was much purring. He gave the cat the second can before going into microwave his chicken and Swiss sandwich.

Arthur then did something he hadn't considered doing in years: he sat down at his typewriter. He didn't use it but did find the motivation to wind a frighteningly empty piece of paper into his old friend. The keys remained quiet for two hours. He finally typed a single word, Monday.

"That'll do for now," he said and went to bed. The day had started much earlier than he would have liked. Though he only had one class the next day, he sensed that Wen would find him. She was vastly easier to tolerate when rested...or so he assumed.

Sometime during the night a storm came up. Something woke him, and he got up. The clock said the bars had just closed, and he heard a little sound outside. "Okay, you can stay here tonight, but don't get any funny ideas."

Arthur was pretty sure he would need to do some shopping for his new roommate because, much like Wen, the little black feline seemed unwilling to listen to reason. He patted the kitten on the head and said, "I'll be calling you Maltese. It suits you. Sleep well, little one." He left Maltese on the couch and went back to bed.

Chapter Ten

Arthur grabbed the phone and looked at the screen. He wasn't surprised. "I may not know much about this terrible thing you've made me buy, but I do know how to use it to tell time. Why would you be calling me at 7:38 am on a Thursday?"

"I've already been running. It is a beautiful day out, and I thought an early start might be a good idea."

"I was having a delightful dream involving several Romanian contortionists doing things that are illegal in a number of highly regarded states. If you hang up now, I might be able to convince them to return to my land of nod."

"We should get together and do some more work on Twitter."

Brian D. Meeks

Arthur rolled onto his back. Out of his peripheral vision he saw that his house guest had decided the couch wasn't fluffy enough. "I've got errands to run."

"What errands?"

"I am out of eggs and coffee, and I was considering finding someone who might be willing to abduct and torture a small Asian woman I know who has wronged me."

"You'll be happy to know that you have 83 followers."

"I'm not sure I'm willing to be their leader. Will I need a flag?"

"Most of them are students, but a few, I think, are readers. Have you checked Twitter today?"

"No, as I said, there were Romanians who were bendy and..."

"Well, you should check now."

"If I promise to look at Twitter and marvel at my meteoric rise to the lofty ranks of high double digits, will you hang up?"

"Do you think I should come over so that we can get to work?"

"I think you should...no, I don't think you should come over. I'm hanging up now. I have stuff to do."

"You want me to help?"

Having gone to bed early, Arthur didn't feel nearly as bad as he did most mornings, but he didn't want to encourage this sort of behavior, so he said, "I'll be fine. You need to make sure that all the TAs run through their class

61

list, find out who has signed up, and, at noon, count the number of people they have followed within the class."

"I know; we've talked about how we're going to do it. Lawrence has a plan that should make it easy."

"That is excellent. Now, I need to go."

"Okay, I'll talk to you later when you aren't such a grumpy pants."

"Fine, I'll be available late July, 2019," he said. He thought he heard her giggle before she hung up.

A tail smacked him on the forehead. "Don't you start."

Maltese purred.

Arthur petted the fur ball and let the sting of morning subside. After ten minutes of kitty time, he was ready to get started.

Two hours later he was placing various feline sundry items in the Triumph. Good deeds were not his way, but the cat seemed to bring a certain level of low-tech to his new high tech world. He would feed the cat, and, on occasion, the little furry mess would do something cute. It was a reasonable exchange of goods for services.

His phone rang.

"Hello," he said, somewhat thankful it wasn't Wen.

"Dr. Byrne, how are you today?"

"I'm fine, and you, Mary?"

"I just wanted to ask that you stop in my office for a little chat after your class today."

"How did you get this number? I just got the phone."

"We need to discuss your antics yesterday. I'm afraid I have some very disturbing reports."

"Did you get them from Wen?"

"Very disturbing reports. Your attitude reflects poorly on this school and on me as dean. Are you trying to embarrass me?"

"One of the features I do like on this phone is..." and he hung up on her. Arthur turned the key and was greeted with a feeble attempt at starting. He shrugged and tried again. Nothing. "Damn you, karma. If I promise to never do anything nice again, will you please start the fucking car?"

Karma didn't respond.

Arthur, remembering what Wen had said about the woman that lives in his phone, asked Siri for a tow truck. She suggested Dwayne's Towing.

Chapter Eleven

The shirt and truck both had "Dwayne" written on them. Arthur said, "You must be Dwayne."

"Yes, sir," he said looking at the car. "She's a beauty. What's the trouble?"

"She is giving me grief...women."

Dwayne laughed. "You mind popping the hood?"

"Not at all."

Dwayne seemed to give his baby a good physical. Arthur knew less about the workings of his car than he did about the internet.

Dwayne said, "I'm not sure, but one of the battery cables is a little loose." A few minutes later, he said, "Try it now."

Arthur turned the key and his charming little car struggled then started. He got out and shook Dwayne's hand. "Thanks so much. I'm glad it wasn't anything serious."

Brian D. Meeks

"No problem."

"How much do I owe you?"

"I was actually driving right past here on the way to the shop, so your timing couldn't have been better. How does ten bucks sound?"

"It sounds low. Let's say twenty. Do you take plastic?"

"Sure do. I don't think I've ever had anyone negotiate up," he said, looking at the card. "Are you any relation to the author?"

"It depends upon who you're thinking about."

"There's a writer, Arthur Byrne."

"Then yes."

"I picked up your book a few years back. Nice job."

"You are too kind."

"You have anything new coming out?" he asked, handing back the card.

"No, now I mostly just teach. It is what one does when one forgets how to write."

"I doubt you've forgotten. I bet you just have a loose battery cable."

"Dwayne, you should be the writer. And thanks again."

Maltese seemed interested in his return. Three loud meows told Arthur that the cat wanted to investigate the food first. The toys could wait. While his guest dined, he set up the litter box in the back bedroom and put the scratching post under the table with his typewriter.

65

He had been thinking about getting a plant for a few years. This was better. The cat squared away, Arthur headed to campus. It was too nice a day to drive, so he walked. He dreaded the meeting with Mary and decided he wasn't the least bit interested in her time table.

Her secretary said, "You're not expected until..."

"Nobody expects the Spanish Inquisition," and he blew past her, knocked twice, and entered.

The dean was reading some reports and looked up. She removed the reading glasses from her beak and made a show of cleaning the lenses. She didn't invite him to sit. With a squint of derision, she said, "Our meeting isn't scheduled until..."

"I was in the neighborhood, smelled baked goods, and thought I'd check out the gingerbread house. I was told not to eat anything or the..." he paused. "Well, rumor has it the punishment is severe."

"The only thing more grim than your sense of humor is the disgusting display you put on for your first day of class."

"I got an ovation."

She shook several pieces of paper and said, "I had a few people look on, and the overwhelming majority of the reports were negative. Shall I read you some of the comments?"

"I'll wait until the Cliff's Notes come out."

"I quote, 'He was sitting among the students and began ranting like a lunatic.'"

Arthur started typing something on his phone.

She tried to ignore his rudeness and continued, "And then it was reported that you, 'showed disregard for the scheduled class time by leaving early...' What are you doing? Would you mind NOT texting while we are having a discussion?"

"I'm not texting; I'm tweeting."

"Then please stop tweeting. You can do that on your own..."

"When one is using a hashtag, is #StickUpAss spelled with two spaces or none?"

She stood, resisted the urge to yell, and said with suppressed rage, "I'll have you know that you are officially on probation and..."

Arthur stood. "Oh, that is good news. I was afraid I might be on double secret probation. Well, if that is all, I've got dozens of tweets to get out...hashtag h...a...g." He left.

As he walked past the secretary, he said, "I think she is on the cusp of a massive stroke. If I were you I'd call someone...or take an early lunch. Bon appetit."

Arthur returned to his office where he found Kurt waiting and asked, "Good morning, Kurt, how are you?"

"I'm well, thanks."

"How may I help you?"

"I have a class at noon, and we were supposed to go through our students' Twitter accounts to figure out how many points they each got."

Arthur shrugged, "Do it afterwards. If there's an inquisition, I'll say you had a moment of temporary insanity."

Kurt smiled and said, "Okay, thanks. I didn't think it was a big deal, but I wanted to make sure."

"Have you looked at the numbers to see how they're doing?"

"Yes, it looks like most of the students have followed everyone who followed you, but I'm only to count the people who are in the class, right?"

"How many people do I have following me?"

"Just over 130."

"But there are only 104 in the class...is that right?" Arthur said, unsure.

"Yes, but you also have us TAs and you've gotten some spammers and Keyboard Cat."

"I'm being followed by a musical cat?"

"You don't know Keyboard Cat?" Kurt asked, shocked. "He's a YouTube sensation. Here, look." Kurt handed his phone to Arthur. He started to bob his head to the music.

"Is this the sort of thing you young people enjoy?"

"It's awesome. Don't YOU like it?"

"I laughed, I cried, I lost several IQ points...which is upsetting because I tend to prefer to spend those on drink."

"Whatever."

"I should probably spend some time surfing the world-wide web. Dean Wormer has it out for me."

"Who?"

"Nobody. Don't you know Animal House?"

"Ah...no, sorry. Was it by George Orwell?"

There was a long pause. "Steve, it warms my heart that you thought I was talking about a book, and, admittedly, that was a good guess. If you'd like, I'll be happy to stop calling you Kurt. Literary references earn bonus points... for the record."

"All the TAs call me Kurt now. I've never had a nick-name before, and it is sort of cool. I'll stick with Kurt."

"Fair enough."

Kurt stood up and headed out. Arthur smiled to himself and opened a browser on his computer. It was time to embrace his reality.

Chapter Twelve

Arthur sat at his computer. He had, after much fidgeting and procrastination, successfully logged into his Twitter account. There were more than a few comments directed to him, mostly from students who thought the first day of class was better than most.

It seemed rude not to respond, so he typed, "Thanks, see you Friday morning," or some variation to most of the students. Now, faced with a blank 140 character canvas, he wanted to send out a real tweet. What to write?

It wasn't just a question of tweeting; it was THE question that had been plaguing him for over a decade. Damn, why is this so hard? 140 characters does not a novel make! He decided to go with "What is the sexiest root vegetable? Enquiring minds want to know."

It took five minutes before he hit the send button.

That done, he sat and waited. He didn't know for what, but he expected something to happen. The silence spoke only of loneliness. A few tweets were added to the stream. One had a snarky political comment that made him chuckle. He didn't respond.

Another tweet had a hashtag that read #ScottishLust with a link. One didn't need to be a social media guru to know it was probably a bad idea to click on the link.

A few more tweets appeared in rapid succession. They were between two students talking about football. Arthur wanted to jump in, but it seemed like he would be intruding. He loved football. Though Arthur wasn't enough of a sports junkie to hang with the most rabid fans, football was fun to discuss. He wrote down on his yellow pad, "Is it okay to jump into a conversation?"

He would ask Wen or Kurt later.

The next tweet had a link to an old blog post on a site called Spin Sucks. Arthur had to agree that spin did, as a matter of fact, suck. He clicked on the post and began to read. It had a quote in the beginning that Arthur liked: "The pen is mightier than the sword" by Edward Bulwer-Lytton from Richelieu. Arthur was hooked.

He read on, "If this is true, and I believe it is, then the combination of the keyboard (21st century pen) when combined with tweeting, would kick Edward's pen's ass.

Sure there will be skeptics. I get that. There is a sport, which is known by some, but perfected by few. I speak, of course, of #fakehashtaggery. It is usually played on a platform such as Tweetdeck or Hootsuite, though one could certainly use Twitter. Does anybody use Twitter for tweeting anymore? I digress."

Arthur didn't understand the bit about anyone using Twitter for tweeting anymore. He wrote it down as another question and went back to the post. He finished reading and called Wen. He sensed a bit of excitement deep in his funny bone, and he had to share.

"Hello, Dr. Byrne, how's it going?"

"I'm doing some research. I'm reading a blog post on Spin Sucks."

"You know Spin Sucks?"

"Somebody tweeted a link."

"I love that site."

"Well, have you read the post on fake hashtaggery?"

"I don't think so."

"It is older, from...just a second...March 29, 2011."

"I'll check it out."

"I've got it up, let me read this to you."

* * *

"The sport of #fakehashtaggery dates back thousands of years to 2009.

"To those readers who have been using Twitter for a while, I don't need to explain that the pound sign is also called a hashtag. To those who haven't been using Twitter until recently, please stop reading, go sit in the corner, and think about what you have done. Oh, don't try to play dumb. I know you mocked Twitter relentlessly until you started to see tweets on the CNN crawler. Then, all of a sudden, it was okay. Well, some of us have been here for years. We have been airing our grievances, 140 characters at a time, all to build a world where people can search for loved ones in a disaster or overthrow a dictator. You're welcome.

"This brings me back to the most exciting sport since Bulgarian Ratapult. #fakehashtaggery is played by one or thousands. It often starts when a twelve-year-old girl tweets something like 'Justin Bieber is the greatest musician EVER.'

"The first salvo would go something like this: '@Sally021999 No, he isn't. He sounds like a cat producing a pile of sick. #BieberIsAMonkeyFacedBoy'

"The little biebette might respond, but this only makes it worse. '@Sally021999 His lyrics are trite. Your parents don't love you. #BieberHairSucks'

"If she isn't crying by now, then it is hard to say which way it will go. She will either log off Twitter or, and this is where #fakehashtaggery can become dangerous, she might rally several thousand screeching preteens to her cause. This can quickly turn into millions of people, all berating one's middle aged baldness and lack of fashion sense. This is not a game for the faint of heart.

"Few people know that Mubarak once tweeted that 'David Hasselhoff was overrated and that Baywatch sucked.' Within minutes, a gang of ruthless German tweeple was using hashtags to imply an improper relationship between the President and a farm animal in a bikini. Twenty minutes later, he stepped down and he hasn't been seen tweeting since.

"Now don't get me wrong, hashtags are very useful. I like to set up a search using #reading or #writing to find kindred spirits. Hashtags, when used properly, are very handy for group discussions. They make Twitter fun, can help with promoting, and as I have said, even aid in emergencies. I don't mock the hashtag itself. But there are days when I am feeling a little #snarky and a round or two of #fakehashtaggery really lifts my spirits."

 · ° · ° · ° · ° · ° ·

Wen was laughing when Arthur got to the end. She chirped, "That's funny. See, the internet isn't so bad now, is it?"

"It has gotten me thinking about all the crap I said during my first-day rant."

"You were great."

74

"I was making up stuff as I went along, but maybe some of it was a good idea?"

"I thought all of it was..."

"Okay, tamp down the unbridled enthusiasm for a moment and stay with me. Had we planned on doing anything with blogging?"

"Yes, it's in the syllabus. Haven't you read it?"

"You are allowed one stupid question per day, and that was it. I mean, in the few days we've known each other, what led you to believe I might actually read the syllabus?"

"Momentary bout of optimism?"

"Hopefully, I'll be able to browbeat that sunny disposition out of you by mid-term. Now, how about we require everyone to start a blog? Are they expensive?"

"No, there are free ones like Blogger."

Arthur wrote down Blogger. "Can anyone blog on Blogger?"

"Sure."

"Excellent. Is it hard to set up?"

"Well..."

"Well what?"

"It would take me about five minutes."

"How long would it take me?"

"Maybe somewhere between six minutes and 'I quit; this is stupid; let's go to the bar.'"

75

"Well done, Lou, you HAVE been paying attention. That had an edge to it. Give yourself a high five later."

"Okay," she said with a light giggle.

"I'm going to try to figure out how to set up a free blog. If it's hard, I'm blaming you."

"Good luck, Dr. Byrne."

Arthur bravely typed "Blogger" into Google. It would take him ten minutes to set up. It was then that he realized the flaw in his plan: blogging is writing even if it is the most lowly form.

Chapter Thirteen

"Is it warm in the lecture hall today?" Arthur asked.

Wen asked, "Do you want me to check?"

"No, that's all right. If you could get those people playing the gongs to stop, that would be wonderful, Lou."

"Gongs?"

"Never mind. I'm heading out into the fray."

The chatter quieted, and Arthur said, "It looks like we are closer to having a full class here today. I hope everyone is well?"

It seemed they were. Arthur sensed he was the only one not enthused about being there. "So, by a show of hands, how many of you set up new Twitter accounts?"

"That's interesting, it seems that not only did our Wednesday attendees do their homework, but so did those who were otherwise engaged on the first day of class. Well done. Have you been using your accounts?"

Most of the hands went up.

Arthur spent some time talking about the value of getting into a habit. He rambled for a while about some things he had read on various blog posts and read the post about fake hashtags. It was well received. Thirty minutes of the fifty remained. He was out of material.

A student asked a question, which thankfully, Wen jumped in and took. Arthur then asked, "How many of you read one or more blogs on a regular basis?"

He was surprised by how few people actually read blogs. "Have you considered the power of citizen media?" he asked. It was rhetorical because he was sure they hadn't. He was also confident he had not considered it, either.

He tried a pensive look, with some pacing, but it only used five seconds. It was time to talk again. His brain was screaming something about the hair of the dog but suggesting they adjourn to the bar seemed to be crossing a line that even Arthur knew was a step too far.

He had never had speaker's block. "I'm surprised that so few of you read blogs. It seems to be all the rage, and I assumed this class was hip. I guess we will need to adapt. I'm nothing if not flexible. You, the young man with the questionable hair cut, what are you studying?"

"I'm in the journalism department."

"Do you read blogs?"

"Not regularly. Sometimes I read The Huffington Post, which is sort of a blog."

"You like to write about current events though?"

"Yes, I love it, and I always read the paper."

"And how are newspapers doing in our fair country?"

"Not very well."

"Not very well at all. I want you to find three blogs that write about news you're interested in and leave comments. Then, copy and paste the articles in a word document, hit print, and bring the paper to class. Can you do that?"

"Sure."

"You all have dreams, and it is partly my job to crush them like a grape...oh, wait...that doesn't sound right. What was I saying? Oh, yes, there are blogs about everything under the sun. If you are studying graphic art, find a blog about that, if you love business, then...well, you see where I'm going with this. Now, don't think you can find a post and write, "Nice post; loved it," and expect it won't be met with a healthy dose of red ink and a scornful look from your TAs. Lou, give them a scornful look."

Wen did her best, but scornful wasn't her forte. It was more of an angry bear cub, and there were almost as many "aw's" as chuckles.

"Now, some of you said you read blogs," he said walking to the blackboard. "Let's hear them?"

People started shouting out various sites, and Arthur wrote them down. The spellings were strange enough that his plan worked to perfection. It took nearly twenty minutes to fill up the board. Students furiously copied down the urls. It really seemed like he was teaching a class on social media.

He wasn't quite to fifty minutes, so he asked a couple of people what the blogs they read were about. Their answers, thankfully, were somewhat longwinded. Class ended. Arthur disappeared back stage and slumped into a chair.

Lawrence found him and said, "Good class."

"Thanks. Did it seem like I was faking it?"

"Well, maybe, but the blog reading was a good idea."

Kurt said, "I agree."

"That it was obvious I was faking it, or the blog reading was a good idea?"

"Yes."

"I really do need to step up my game for next week."

Wen said, "I think you did fine."

"I think I'll head to my office and spend some time tweeting."

Wen cocked her head and said, "Are you really?"

"When I say tweeting, I may not be speaking in strictly literal terms." Arthur got up and, without another word, left.

His secretary took one look at him and handed over the bottle of aspirin. Eric walked in and said, "You look a little rough."

"I know, but it's nothing a little couch time can't fix. What's up?"

Eric followed Arthur back to his office and said, "We didn't see you at the Pit last night."

"Did you use the personal pronoun 'we'?"

"Emily and I."

"Since when did you become a 'we'?"

"We're not a 'we' yet, but I'm taking her to dinner tonight."

"Isn't she a little old for you?"

"I'm 38, but I don't think she's much older."

"Well, good for you. She's nice looking and smart, if you're into that sort of thing."

"I am. Where do you think I should take her?"

"I think you should get dating advice from someone who goes on dates."

"Do you think Italian would be too aggressive a choice?"

"I don't know what that means."

"The Italian place is pretty nice. Does it say I'm hoping to get lucky?"

"You are hoping to get lucky."

"Yes, but I don't want it to be obvious."

"She's smart and nice looking. I'm sure you're not the first guy to ask her out."

"I know. Maybe Chinese food?"

"How about dog food? You could go to the pet store. Chicks dig puppies."

"You're not helpful."

"I'm many things. Helpful is not among them. Don't you have a class to teach or a diary entry to fill with tiny hearts?"

"She's really amazing. After college, Emily spent two years studying in France then lived in Russia for a year. We talked about Rodin. Not just 'The Thinker' but the 'Balzac' piece and the 'Burghers of Calais.'"

"You are smitten."

"I really am. You need to hang out with us. I think you would like her."

"Maybe I can be the third wheel when you go to the prom?"

"I do have a class. I'll talk to you later."

"Text me and let me know what she says when you give her your letter jacket." Arthur flopped down on the couch and yelled, "I'm not here." He went to sleep thinking about Rodin. Arthur liked 'The Burghers of Calais,' too.

Chapter Fourteen

Arthur looked at both ends of the couch, but sleep was nowhere to be found. He gave up.

An hour of swimming about in the shallow waters of the internet on sites like CNN and Yahoo did nothing to change Arthur's low opinion of the human race and society in general. A link caught his eye. It led to another. Before he knew it, there was an article about a new phone prototype.

When he was done reading the article that talked about a transparent phone, he screamed, "Are you kidding me?"

The door flew open, "What is it? Are you okay?"

"I'm fine. Actually, no, I'm not. Look at this," he said pointing to the screen.

"A see-through phone. Huh, I'm not sure I see the point."

"That is why I screamed."

"I'm not sure I see the point of screaming, either."

"How do I get paper on this thing?"

"Do you mean you want to write something?"

"Yes."

She took the mouse and brought up Microsoft Word and said, "See the little disk in the corner? That is how you save. If you need help, let me know. This is quite a leap forward for you. I'm impressed."

Arthur waved his hand, and she walked out. He began to type.

"I admit that I've nurtured my tech phobia since before the word 'tech' was even used, but today I read about something that has me hotter than a summer day in Death Valley.

"It seems that a company in Tokyo has developed a prototype of a phone that is see-through. It's clear plastic, and, when it is off, it is nothing more than clear plastic. Well, whoop-de-doo!

"I don't know how many hours they've spent developing this technology, but I'd wager it wasn't inexpensive. I'd guess it cost well over five dollars, which I think would have been better spent on a cup of coffee. Now, charging five bucks for hot water poured over beans is crazy but only marginally less so than the people (myself) who pay the ridiculous price. I digress.

"Why would being able to see through your phone be important? It isn't a trick question; I want to know. Oh, sure, maybe it will be 'cool,' but there are plenty of things that are cool.

There are plenty of things that SHOULD be transparent. Politicians come to mind, but no amount of research, technology, or money is going to create one of those. I played poker with a guy back in college whose bluffs redefined transparent. He paid for my junior year.

"I remember a woman in New York. I think her name was Sally or Susan or Hottie McHotterson, but the name isn't important. I think I was fourteen at the time. She had long legs, high cheek bones, and breasts that were hidden behind a blouse that I spent many summer evenings wishing was transparent. The day I saw the advertisement in the back of a comic book for x-ray glasses, I felt like I had found the Rosetta Stone.

"I did odd jobs for two solid weeks to make enough money to send away for the glasses. It was hard work. When they arrived, well, let's just say that Hottie McHotterson remained un-gawked. It was a dark day indeed. It's been 39 years since that disappointing package arrived. Surely, given almost four decades, the scientists who wasted their time developing a phone you could see through could have spent the time making the dreams of teenage boys come true? Isn't that a better use of resources?

"That is our problem as a species: we don't think. I'm not a rocket scientist; I'm not even a rocket enthusiast, but can't we spend less time developing useless crap and more time solving problems like housing in third-world countries, water pollution, and hangovers?

"If I'm wrong, please explain. I'll be glad to make a public apology to all of the needy people who are suffering through their dull lives without being able to see the palm of their hand as they play on their smartphones. I'll even buy you a five dollar cup of brown water."

Arthur lifted his hands from the keyboard. The screen stared back, expressionless. It didn't have the personality of his typewriter. There wasn't any triumphant zip as the last page was yanked from the carriage. It just sat there.

"What do I do now?" he said barely above a whisper. On one hand, he literally didn't know what to do. Arthur wanted to see his words on paper but had no idea how to get them from the screen to a piece of twenty-pound white. On the other hand, he had just written. His stomach churned at the thought...or was it the late night?

The clock, old and familiar, showed that he clearly had a few hours before his next class. He read the rant again. Without warning, the very same clock leapt forward, and it was fifteen minutes until noon. He grabbed his briefcase and walked out.

"Mrs. Putzier, there is something on the screen. Would you mind using your considerable computer prowess to see that it gets onto a piece of dead tree?"

"It was awfully quiet in there. Did you get some rest?"

"Do I look that bad?"

"You've looked worse."

"Thanks."

The class was only two buildings down, so he had plenty of time. He pulled his phone out and brought up the Twitter app. There was a tweet from a woman named @ Nikki_R. He read it, " I admire Emily Dickinson staying alone her whole life, yet she wrote passionately of life and love. I wonder how lonely she must have been."

Arthur, still full of see-through phone angst, slowly typed a reply. "How do you know she was lonely? Not all who are alone are lonely, and not all who are together are loved." He didn't hit send, though. He wasn't sure who the woman was because he didn't remember following her.

He studied Twitter and saw he was following close to 130 people. He hit contacts, found Wen, and was confused for a moment. He touched her number, and the phone started calling. She answered. "Lou, have you been messing around with my Twitter account?"

"Yes, I hope you don't mind, but it seemed rude not to follow your students back, so I went ahead and did it for you."

"That is a valid observation. Who is Nikki?"

"Oh, yes, well, she is someone who followed you. Some of her tweets were interesting and about books, so I thought you would want to follow."

"You are aware that I don't really care for people."

"Oh, you are just saying that."

"Would it be more believable if I tweeted it?"

"If you want I can unfollow her."

"No, it's all right," he said then explained his quandary about whether he should reply. Wen explained that it was exactly the sort of thing he should do on Twitter.

Arthur hit send and climbed the stairs to his classroom.

Chapter Fifteen

The last class seemed to drag. One of his students was more knowledgeable about James Joyce than he found helpful and rambled on until finally Arthur had needed to cut him off. It didn't matter because his mind wasn't on books; it was back with his writing.

If there was one thing he took pride in, it was his seriousness with which he treated the literature classes he taught. There were pangs of guilt at how he had "mailed it in." He planned to do better next week, but for now, he wanted to talk about what had happened.

Arthur called Eric, but his phone went to voice mail. It didn't seem like the sort of thing he wanted to leave as a message, so Arthur hung up. He walked from class to the union and got a bagel.

The cream cheese was delicious. He tuned out the inane chatter of the bubbly youth all around, so he didn't hear the student at first until she said, "I'm sorry; I'll leave you alone, Dr. Byrne."

"What, oh, I was a million miles away. What can I do for you?"

"I'm in your SMS 301 class," she said, not making eye contact.

"Please, have a seat."

She wore a big, pink Hello Kitty back pack, had jet black hair, wore what looked like a large t-shirt that seemed a little snug, and smelled like peaches. "I really don't want to interrupt."

Arthur laughed and said, "If you only knew of the trivial, idle thoughts that were accompanying my bagel...anyway, I'm happy to chat."

"I liked the first day of class, and today was even better. I'm sort of shy. It was really hard to sign up for Twitter and following all those people...well, that was awful."

"I'm sorry you felt that way."

"Oh, I did, but I'm not done. I only had one friend in high school, and he went to USC. We talk all the time and chat on Facebook, but it is still sort of lonely. Now that I'm a junior, though, the reality of life after college is starting to frighten me some. It can be scary out there."

"I've been out there, and that's why I came back here."

The grin said more than her words. "Anyway, my fear of missing out on points was greater than my fear of meeting new people, so I followed everybody that followed you that first night and then kept following as the next morning went on. I think I got everyone by the cut-off."

"Well done!"

"I tweeted hello to the world and a picture of my dog, Barney, who is awesome. Did you see it?"

"I may have missed that one."

"It's okay because two other people saw it and RTed the picture. They both said he was very cute, and we started talking. It is weird having a conversation when you can't go over 140 characters."

"Yes, it is," Arthur said, trying to sound knowledgeable.

"It was awesome. I am self-conscious because of my weight, but on Twitter people can't see me. I used a picture, but that is okay; I like my hair like this. The point is I've been chatting and tweeting with people a bunch since yesterday. When I got to class, I was suddenly mortified because I realized they would all be right there, too."

Arthur was starting to get worried. He hadn't considered there might be a downside to his first assignment.

"As soon as I walked in the door, Jennifer, the first person who RTed the Barney photo...oh, wait, I've got it right here," she said, holding up a picture of her Scottish Terrier.

"Barney IS adorable."

"Anyway, Jennifer saw me as soon as I walked in and waved me over. Phil found us, too, and we all sat together.

It was so weird. I hadn't known them very long, but it was like we had been friends for...well...longer than two days. I already knew that Phil studies geology, is from Maine, and likes chocolate, and Jennifer studied abroad for a year in France. Today after class, we went and got coffee."

"That's a great story."

"I've never been good at making friends, or at least that is what I thought. I like to talk, but I'm always afraid. It turns out that Twitter lets you find people who like the same things, and it isn't scary."

"Now, that may be true, but you always want to be careful about trusting too much of people online - not to be a downer."

"Oh, I know, but these people were already students here. I could have just as easily met them over a...bagel," she said with just a glint in her eye. " I wanted to thank you. Loneliness isn't so bad or noticeable after a while, but when you make a new friend, it's sort of awesome. I have to go. Jennifer, Phil and I are getting together to find some blog posts. I'm bringing cookies," she said with a grin.

With that, the heavy, little goth girl seemed to float away. Arthur, over the years, had spent countless hours talking to starry-eyed students or, more aptly, talking about himself to them as an adoring audience. He wasn't sure if he had ever spoken with them. Damn, I didn't get her name.

Arthur tossed his empty cream cheese container and napkin in the garbage. His mind was spinning as he replayed the story. He couldn't remember the last time he really needed NOT to drink.

Arthur did the math. If he called for Chinese food, they would arrive a few minutes after he got home. When he arrived inside the door, the little furry guest, which he had not thought about all day, would bound from the top of the couch and start doing laps between his legs. A quiet Friday night with Maltese the cat and some steamed dumplings was exactly what he needed.

Chapter Sixteen

Maltese found a spot on Arthur's chest, which was fine; he didn't mind. It was hard to tell what time it was and opening the old peepers to check seemed like a terrible idea. The soft purr was a great way to start the day.

The bat on the nose, though, was a bit of a surprise.

"I didn't see that coming. Good morning, tiny, fuzzy one. Do you want something?"

"Meow," Maltese said in perfect cat.

"I can only assume that means 'feed me because I've just gotten up and there is a nap on my schedule for which I'd rather not be late.'"

Maltese stood, stretched, and walked out of the bedroom.

The light leaking across the hard wood floor was warm. It looked unfamiliar. Arthur checked the clock. "6:40 am?! Why would you get me up at this horrible hour?"

Maltese didn't answer but sat by his bowl. He was as still as a raven on a bust above a chamber door. "You will be getting me out of bed at this hour nevermore."

Arthur poured the food in the bowl and changed the water. Morning and he had never been friends. He didn't feel hungover, but a night off from drinking wasn't treating him as well as he might have liked.

His internal voice wanted to know when they were going to the bar. Just bringing up the subject, especially in a rare state of micro-sobriety, was more than disturbing; it was telling. He wasn't proud of his daily alcohol consumption, but his sentiment didn't rise to the level of shame, either.

There had always been a part of him that suspected this day might come. How long can one be miserable before it loses its appeal? The first day wasn't the problem, but he knew there was a fair amount of unpleasantness coming if he should choose to ignore the wishes of his mind and body. They would likely retaliate.

He feared self-confrontation.

Come on, Arthur, change the subject. You did something yesterday that was worth thinking about. Of course, I mean the writing, but that goth girl was sort of neat, too. Let's think about them, not the tiny glass and the delightful sound of the ice cubes being dropped to the bottom. Don't romanticize it; call it what it is, a life distraction.

Underwood, Scotch, and Wry

He almost called Eric, but it was only seven o'clock. The coffee pot, which hadn't been used in a long time, seemed inviting. There wasn't any coffee or filters.

Maltese had finished eating and curled up on the couch to nap. "Bastard!"

He had to leave, go somewhere, do something. Arthur fixed his mind on the idea of grocery shopping. Are groceries open now? It didn't matter; that was where he was heading. If they were closed, maybe he would just wait.

By ten o'clock, his refrigerator had filled to a level that was satisfying to regard. Arthur stood with the door open, something that would not have gone unnoticed by his mother were she within a ten mile radius. All that food and yet, he didn't have much of an appetite.

Maltese was interested in some attention, so Arthur picked up the cat. With feline and phone in hand, he eased into the chair that had been a faithful companion since he signed his first book deal.

There was still an internal battle going on, and his mind was making a convincing argument for libations. He needed a distraction. The phone had just such a distraction. He hadn't opened it before, so he hit the app that Wen had decided he needed.

The instructions were clear, and he started to play. The first level was easy and, he had to admit, fun. Level two wasn't bad, either, but he soon was playing level eight and got stumped but only for a minute.

Maltese went to sleep on his lap and only looked up briefly when the phone rang. Arthur said, "Lou, how you doing?"

"Did I wake you?"

"Always a reasonable assumption, and I may be on the cusp of a nap, but no, I was just sitting here messing with Avian Angst."

There was quiet and a squeal, "You mean Angry Birds! I got one of your jokes," she said. Arthur could feel the rays of smile-shine coming through the phone.

"I'll need to try harder to be obscure."

"Do you love it?"

"I don't hate it."

"I'm glad."

"So, how can I help you?"

"I just wanted to see how you were doing. Have you tweeted today?"

"Don't you follow me on Twitter?"

"Yes."

"So you know the answer to that, don't you?"

"Okay, you caught me."

"You are right to be concerned, and I should probably keep trying to figure out why all the kids are so excited about social media."

"You need any help?"

"I really don't want to walk all the way to the office, though. I can't believe that in one tiny week, I've become one of those people who works on the weekends. I hate those people."

"So, you are thinking you need to go into the office, but you would rather not?"

"That about sums it up."

"You know, I was reading a blog post the other day. It was really interesting. I think you might like it. It seems, and I can't say I checked the writer's credentials, but she seemed knowledgeable...anyway, it seems that there has been a huge breakthrough in technology and some people have...again, you may not believe me and I can send you the link if you don't...but she said some people have started to get computers in their homes. Crazy, I know, but..."

"Wow, not even a week has passed and already you have learned to wield sarcasm...and with such a deft touch. I never saw it coming. You are like a sarcasm ninja. Is that racist? Maybe, but well done, grasshopper...which is also probably racist and I doubt a reference..."

"I love David Carradine...but I don't think I'm ready to walk the rice paper...old master...was that ageist?..Maybe, but..."

"Okay, I yield. You think you know a place where a guy could pick up one of these fancy new-fangled home computators?"

"I do."

"You mind taking me shopping, again?"

"I'm on my way."

Chapter Seventeen

The TR3 hummed along. Arthur asked, "So this place, it has good computers?"

"They have everything. The best part is they're local."

"Supporting a mom-and-pop business is an honorable thing to do."

"A secret person works there, and he's working today. He knows a ton about computer hardware, and I thought you would be more comfortable buying from him than from one of the blue shirts."

"Definitely...what's a blue shirt? And who's the secret person?"

"It's not important. Turn right at the corner and again into the lot of that strip mall."

He whipped the car into a spot near the street where he was confident nobody would ding his darling. They walked in and saw Kurt helping a woman and her daughter. There was an older man with a young guy at the register and a woman of similar age was showing a printer to a man who looked like he might be just as intimidated by tech as Arthur.

"Lou, what do you think I should get?"

"I like laptops, but desktops are nice, too, especially if you are a gamer. Are you a gamer?" she said with a devilish smile.

"I have an arsenal of ill-tempered fowl, and I'm not afraid to use them. Don't make me fling one of the exploding ones at you."

"Hey, he's free. Let's go."

Kurt saw them, "Well, I surely didn't expect to see you here, Dr. Byrne."

"It's the weekend. You can call me Arthur...or, I suppose, to be fair, anything you like."

"I'm not very good at making up clever nicknames, so how may I help you?"

"I've decided to embrace technology and submit myself to her evil, time-sucking siren's call."

"You sound like a gamer...well, a gamer with a flair for language."

"I am a gamer!"

Kurt cocked his head. "Do tell?"

Wen laughed. "He has been playing Angry Birds. What level are you on?"

"I've made it through level eight and am sure one of the greatest bird-flinging strategists to have ever walked the earth."

"There's like a million levels," said Kurt.

"And each of them shall feel my wrath."

"Well, then we better get you set up. Apple or PC?"

"I have an Apple phone. Does that matter?"

"You can synch with either type, but Apples are nice." Kurt showed Arthur a sexy looking machine and talked at length about all the stuff one could do on it. Arthur listened and tried to take in the techno babble as much as he could. He was making a genuine effort.

Arthur asked, "What is that over there? Does it have two monitors?"

"Keen eye, Dr. B. Oh, I like that, I think I'll call you Dr. B. Is that all right?"

"It works for me. Do you earn commission?"

"I do, but I promise I'll..."

"Oh, I know you will. I was just curious. So, tell me about the two-headed monster."

"This really is a gaming computer but, all joking aside, having two screens would give you a lot of space for doing social media stuff."

Arthur liked the look of it and moved the mouse over one of the few things he recognized, the browser icon. He clicked and it opened up with the computer store's home page. Kurt's phone rang.

"I can't talk now, sweetie, I'm with someone," he said and paused, "Don't be silly. I meant at work. I'm with a customer. Don't be such a diva." He hung up. "Sorry, he's doing a show tonight and is all freaked out."

Wen said, "His boyfriend is a drag queen."

Arthur said, "Cool. Now, what sort of stuff comes on this bad boy?"

Kurt asked, "You're letting that one go?"

"I have to admit that I'm sure there's some sort of great shot I could take, but I wasn't prepared for the gay guy dating a guy who dresses like a girl. That's pure gold, but I drew a blank. I must be off my game."

"That's okay. Maybe you can think of something later and get back to me."

"That's sporting of you; I do hate to pass up such a gem."

"He really is a diva, though, but let's not lose focus. You're here to buy a computer. What do you think?"

"Lou, what do you think?"

"It is a sweet machine. If you ever did want to get into FPS or MMORPG, this would make you a bad ass."

"You took far too much pleasure in showing off that strange alien geek language of yours."

"I really did, but I'm happy to translate. FPS means first person shooter and MMORPG is a massive multi-player online role playing game."

"I don't think I'm ready for that."

Kurt laughed. "He would be the biggest noob ever."

Lou laughed, too, and Arthur knew it was at his expense even if he didn't get the joke. It didn't matter, though; he was truly excited about getting a new toy even if it still scared the shit out of him. "I want this bad boy right here, but I'll need one more thing...a printer."

"We have a great HP printer on sale that would be perfect. I think I can even talk the owner into throwing in a free extra set of ink cartridges," Kurt said and walked off towards the older man.

"So, what do you think, am I being silly buying such a massive computer?"

"No, it is awesome. Since it's completely current, it will last for a long time before you need to upgrade."

"I want it!"

Kurt came back and said, "I told him I could close you if he threw in the extra ink. He agreed."

Arthur put on a serious face, stuck out his hand, and said loud enough so that Kurt's boss could hear, "You drive a hard bargain, but I'll take them both." He paused as he realized his blunder. "I'm not sure I can fit all that in my car. It's tiny."

"I'm off in 30 minutes. I can drop it by your house."

Wen said, "I'll wait until he's off work and help. I'll show him where you live."

Arthur handed Kurt his credit card, "I'll have a massive pizza waiting when you get there. If you want to invite your boyfriend, the more the merrier."

"I'll ask him, but he never eats the day of a show...such a diva."

Arthur left, got in his car, and tweeted, "Just picked up a new computer to keep up with all the cool kids."

Before he got home, it had been retweeted six times.

Chapter Eighteen

Kurt and Wen set up the computer while Arthur paced around the living room. Maltese seemed pleased with the printer box and had curled up inside. "How's it going?" Arthur asked, sounding like an expectant parent.

Kurt smiled. "Worry not, Dr. B, your brand-new, bouncing baby HP is almost ready to take its first breath."

Wen said, "Would you like us to set up your browser, Twitter and everything?'

"Oh, by all means, set up everything. Scan the Internet far and wide for all that might intrigue or inspire."

Kurt said, "So porn then?"

"Good God, no, I can't imagine having any of that wretched filth on my lovely new computer...maybe just a little."

Kurt laughed and Wen did, too, though more nervously.

"I jest, fair Lou. You may put whatever is normal and respectable onto my new toy."

"Here you go, Dr. B, she is all yours."

Arthur sat at the computer and, with nary a sign of trepidation, typed his first home tweet, "My exceedingly able TAs have helped me buy and set up a new computer. Hooray!!!"

Wen, looking over his shoulder, said, "That is a lot of enthusiasm for you."

"I'm feeling puckish."

Kurt grabbed another piece of pizza. "Thanks for the pepperoni and sausage, Dr. B."

"Thanks for escorting me into the modern era. Now what?"

Wen said, "How about we show you Foursquare?"

"I love Foursquare. I'm the Mayor of Tony's Subs," Kurt said around a mouthful of pizza.

"Okay, I had heard of Twitter, but what is Foursquare?"

Wen said, "It's more of a game for your phone, but you can sign up online. Here, give me your phone, and I'll start downloading the app."

When she was done she handed the phone to Kurt.

Kurt helped Arthur sign up for the game and suggested they go try it out. "What do we do?"

"We go to the bars and check in."

"Are you saying that in order to further my social media education, I will need to go to the bars?"

106

"I am."

"If people only knew how I suffered for you students."

Wen said, "Okay, here you go. I've already followed us on your behalf."

Kurt said, "And I've already accepted."

"We follow people on Foursquare, too?"

"We follow people on everything," said Wen with a wink.

"Then I must, in an entirely unsanctioned by the school sort of way, say, to the pub."

Having gone a day without drink, Arthur decided it was best to ease into sobriety with tiny steps and possibly a few stops completely. He would take Sunday and possibly Monday off. Kurt drove because they could all go together.

Arthur bought the first round unofficially, and Wen showed him how to check into the Pit.

The Saturday night crowd was enthusiastically singing along to CCR. Arthur waved as he saw Eric. "Excuse me, my young enablers, but I must go chat with a colleague."

Eric said, "Word on the street is that you were conspicuously absent from the Pit last evening."

"Let the gossips wag their tongues until they turn blue. I've got other news, but I'm sure it pales by comparison to yours. You may begin with the sordid details and work your way back to dinner."

"Dinner was lovely. Emily and I had a nice time."

"You skipped the good stuff. Since when do you hold out on me?"

"I'm not holding out; there is nothing to tell. We had a nice time, and I took her home."

"It is rare that I feel compelled to break out 'balderdash,' but balderdash!"

"You are in high spirits. You rarely go Elizabethan on me anymore, so what is your news?"

"Did you get even so much as a kiss good night and a gentle tug at her ample bosom?"

"What, are we in 18th century high school?"

"Perhaps we are," Arthur said and ordered a scotch.

"We talked. She is very bright and knows a lot about things I enjoy."

"You are being uncharacteristically vague, which can only mean one thing. You blew it."

"I really did."

"What did you do?"

"I think I bored her."

"You bore everyone, but I thought you hit it off so well the other night."

"I thought so, too."

"Maybe it's because you're short. Women don't like short guys. You really should look into getting lengthened."

"They really don't, but I think it was just me."

"I was kidding about the bore thing. You're a charming and educated hobbit-sized man."

"She is taller than me."

"You can't trust tall women."

"I did like her, though."

"Well, let's drink and cast aspersions in her general direction. Barkeep, bring me whiskey for my man here...and beer for my horses."

"So, what is your news?"

"It's a double feature."

"Could I just get the trailers?"

"Sure. I bought a home computer, and I intend to use it."

"That is fantastic on many levels."

"What levels might those be?"

"You really need one, and I've been enduring your mockery of technology for years. Payback is going to be a whole pack of female dogs."

"Ha! And deservedly so. Some of my best snark was over your love of every goddamn gadget that came out. I will gladly take your best shots," he said with a slight bow.

"I'll get back to you, I'm sort of..."

Emily came through the door and spotted them. She came over all smiles and loveliness. "Gentlemen, how are you this evening?"

Arthur said, "I'm dandy. We were just discussing your date."

"We had a nice time. The food was delicious. I wasn't sure if it was a date or not," she said, smiling at Eric. "You didn't even make a move."

Eric said, "You were out of the car pretty quickly."

"I suppose I was. Maybe it was one too many glasses of wine. I had a great time, though," she said and pecked him on the cheek. "Okay, boys, what are we drinking?"

Arthur looked at Eric and Emily and said, "This is a little more festive than the other night."

"I like to start off with demure before I drink my new colleagues under the table like a Russian sailor on shore leave," she said as she flagged down the bartender. "Excuse me, miss, three shots of Grey Goose."

The shots came and went, and some more showed up. When Eric excused himself, Emily turned to Arthur and said, "So, why did you stop writing?"

"Many women have asked me that very question."

"And what did you say?"

"I said, 'Maybe you should get dressed and get back to your boyfriend or husband,' depending upon the circumstances."

"Well, these are entirely different circumstances, aren't they?"

"Are they?"

"I'm wearing all my clothes."

"Yes, and that fact alone puts you at a decided disadvantage."

"Did you just forget how?"

"Yes, that was it."

"I don't believe you."

"I rarely lie...no, that's not true."

"Is there a deep, dark secret?"

"Hardly. Sometimes people run out of ideas is all."

"Bullshit."

"Bovine excrement? Really? And from such a fine-looking Russian sailor."

"Das, bullshit. What's the real reason?"

"What do you think of my fine friend Eric?"

"He's nice," she said and asked, "Does he know why you've quit?"

"He would never tell, well, unless YOU were naked in his bed. Then I imagine he'd give up the launch codes."

"I've read your last book and the articles you did before that. You're a good writer."

"He would probably tell you his bank account routing number, too."

"Admittedly, not as good a writer as you are wingman."

"I'm sure he'd give you his car."

"Fine, I'll figure it out some other way."

Eric returned and asked if he had missed anything. Arthur assured him he had not.

Chapter Nineteen

After an hour at the Pit, Kurt rounded everyone up to go see his boyfriend perform a Beyonce retrospective at "The Good, The Drag, and The Ugly Night." Arthur, who was well-lubricated, found he liked the music but really wanted to talk about spaghetti westerns.

Emily dragged Eric onto the dance floor. Somewhere Fred Astaire rolled in his grave. Wen and Kurt joined them after Arthur refused to be pulled from the table and into the fray.

When "Beyonce" exploded on stage, the crowd went nuts. He did some newer stuff, which Arthur had never heard. All the performers joined him on stage to sing "Bills, Bills, Bills." Even Arthur knew that one.

Arthur admitted, though it was under the influence and not admissible in court, that he had enjoyed himself.

At seven minutes past one in the afternoon, Arthur rolled over and found Maltese curled up but awake. "Hey there."

Maltese said in a non-judgmental way, "Mew." He reached out slowly, put a paw on Arthur's chin, and added a rather long "meow."

"I suspect you're interested in some food, but, before that, how did I get home?'

Maltese didn't seem to know but looked a little concerned.

"Don't worry. I'm fine. This isn't my first Sunday morning, er, afternoon. Let's get you fed and watered...and me, too."

Arthur got out of bed, and Maltese raced to the kitchen. When Arthur caught up, he found the little, black cat sitting patiently next to the bowl. He filled Maltese's bowl with food and made eggs for himself.

Nibbling on toast, Arthur brought up Tweetdeck and watched for a while. He had some more followers and wasn't sure why. Still, it was nice of them to be interested in his musings, so he followed them, too. His first tweet was simply, "How's everyone doing this afternoon?"

A student replied, "Just studying, Dr. Byrne, like every day... ;-)"

He called Wen. "Lou, I'm on Twitter."

"I know. I saw your tweet. I was trying to think of something clever to say in a reply."

"That's why I called. I got a response, and there is some strange punctuation."

"It's probably a typo; that happens with tweets."

"Okay, so semi-colon, dash, right parentheses is an accident?"

She laughed, "Actually, no. That one was intentional. It means 'wink.'"

"How in the world does random punctuation mean wink?"

"It is a sideways smiley face, but the semi-colon makes it look like a wink."

Arthur turned his head and said, "How clever. When did you kids figure that one out?"

"I don't know, but it's not new."

"Does everyone know about this?"

"They do now."

Arthur laughed. "Nice one." He hung up.

A tweet came from Wen, "Happy to help."

Another tweet from a student read, "I'm just watching the Redskins game. You?"

Arthur didn't feel it was appropriate to say something about his hangover to a student, so he wrote back, "Just ate a bit of lunch, well more of a late breakfast, and am going to prep for classes next week."

"Cool. I've already read the assignment and three extra blog posts."

"Well done. Anything interesting?"

"Actually, I just read a hilarious post comparing Snooki and Toni Morrison. Want a link?"

"I can't imagine they have anything in common, but you've piqued my interest. Sure."

A moment later the link showed up, and Arthur clicked on it. A browser window opened, but he didn't start reading immediately.

He got up, started to pace, then called Eric. "Hey, you got a second?"

"Sure, but I'm not giving any details."

"About what? Oh, did you have a sleep-over friend last night?"

"I said I'm not kissing and telling."

"You dawg. Was it that bartender, Craig? I think he dug you."

"Very funny...actually, he was giving me free drinks, no...Emily and I shared a cab, and, well, one thing led to another."

"Did you give her the launch codes?"

"What?"

"Nothing. That isn't why I called, but good for you. No, I just had a conversation with a student."

"Really? You generally don't like to be bothered outside office hours."

"It was on Twitter."

"Who was the student? Is she a hottie?"

"I have no idea, and it was a he."

"Craig?"

Arthur laughed, "I don't think so. I hadn't really gotten the point of Twitter until now. It seemed like a mindless stream of links and inane comments, but, if one wants, one can have a discussion. It is like email or texting, but one doesn't know who is going to show up."

"What do you mean?"

"I asked how people were doing and got some replies, but one of them led to a brief back and forth about school, and the student sent me a link."

"What sort of link?"

"To a blog post he read for his homework. It is a comparison of Snooki and Toni Morrison."

"That sounds hilarious. Was it good?"

"That's what he said, and I don't know. I haven't read it yet."

"What's your Twitter handle?"

Arthur told him. A moment later he had another follower. Arthur asked, "Why do you want to follow me? Don't you get enough of my abuse?"

"Apparently not, but now if you RT the link, I can read the post."

"You're going to read it?"

"Sure, it sounds funny. It sounds like the sort of thing you'd write."

The words were like a fire alarm going off. Arthur had meant to tell Eric that he had written something but had forgotten. Now, in the light of day, he wasn't sure if he wanted to let out his secret. "I'm going to go and give it a read."

"Me, too. Tweet at you later."

Arthur hung up and started to read.

Waxing UnLyrical
April 4th, 2011
"Snooki v. Toni Morrison"

I don't know Snooki. I can say with confidence that I would prefer to be beaten about the head and shoulders with a block of hardened, aged Gouda than to watch 'The Jersey Shore.' And yet, I feel like I want to write a lengthy rant and mock her and the show because of my perceptions. That would be unfair.

It was announced that Snooki will be speaking at a major college on the east coast. She will be receiving $32,000. I applaud her for getting the gig. Toni Morrison, the first black woman to win the Nobel Prize in literature, will also speak. She will receive $30,000.

Underwood, Scotch, and Wry

I have not read anything by Toni Morrison, so I know as much about her as I do Snooki. Shall we take a look at the two of them?

> 'If there's a book that you want to read, but it hasn't been written yet, then you must write it.'
>
> -Toni Morrison

I love that quote. It makes me want to read more of her work.

> 'Everybody google it because that's why the water is salty. Fucking whale sperm.'
>
> -Snooki

I am not a marine biologist, but I think she may have been misinformed. I must admit I didn't google it, though, so I reserve judgment. (I hate that Microsoft Word won't recognize 'google' as a verb. Stupid squiggly lines of judgment. I digress.)

1-0 Toni Morrison takes the lead.

> At some point in life the world's beauty becomes enough. You don't need to photograph, paint, or even remember it. It is enough.'
>
> -Toni Morrison

I am a photographer, so I can't imagine NOT photographing it, but I suspect she is right. It is a fine quote regardless.

> 'I don't go tanning anymore because Obama put a 10% tax on tanning. I feel like he did

that intentionally for us, like McCain would
never put a   10% tax on tanning because
he is pale and would probably wanna be tan.'

-Snooki

Rachael Maddow and Glenn Beck can suck it! This is the sort of in-depth political analysis that this country needs to drag us out of this terrible recession and help choose our leaders.

1-1

'As you enter positions of trust and power,
dream a little before you think.'

-Toni Morrison

This seems wise beyond my ability to comprehend. My gut tells me it's genius, but I suspect that only the Dalai Lama can truly appreciate the quote. I'm sure there are layers and layers to this simple idea. Well done, Toni.

'I don't eat friggin' lobster or anything like
that. Because they're alive when you kill it.'

-Snooki

Maybe she is a marine biologist? Maybe she is a distant cousin of Yogi Berra? Still, the point goes to Toni.

2-1

'We die. That may be the meaning of life. But
we do language. That may be the measure of
our lives.'

-Toni Morrisison

A solid entry. Clearly Toni can tell Snooki is on the ropes. Did she pull her punch?

'Even though we're tiny bitches I don't give a shit. I will fucking attack you like a squirrel monkey.'

-Snooki

I didn't see that one coming, but I laughed. 'Monkey' is always a funny word. Point to Snooki.

"2-2

'Along with the idea of romantic love, she was introduced to another--physical beauty. Probably the most destructive ideas in the history of human thought. Both originated in envy, thrived in insecurity, and ended in disillusion.'

-Toni Morrisison (The Bluest Eyes)

I can see why she won a Nobel prize. That is some fine wordsmithing. Let's see what Snooki has to say in response.

'I am tanned; I like being tanned, BITCH!'

-Snooki

It was a surprisingly close match, but in the end Toni won 3-2.

Aaaarghhh...No. She didn't! Toni Morrison is a national treasure; Snooki is not. There isn't a score card in the galaxy that would read 3-2; it is 5-0 every time. I made it close to keep you reading and for that I apologize. Ms. Morrison won a Nobel in literature; do I need to say it again?

I won't mention the school that deemed Snooki to be $2000 dollars more valuable than Ms. Morrison. Nor will I bash Snooki further as I would gladly take the money, too. I will, however, berate the dregs of society that decided to place a greater value on Snooki than Toni Morrison. I am sure the students will think it is great, because they are the generation who made Snooki, in their own image.

I hope Toni takes her Nobel Prize, melts it down, and fashions a club for beating the stupid out of the attendees. Or at the very least, goes squirrel monkey on them."

Arthur loved it and tweeted to the student, "Thanks, that was fantastic. A good find, indeed."

Another tweet landed on his screen from Eric: "LOL."

Arthur might have been living in the past, but even he recognized that shorthand.

Chapter Twenty

Dean Mary Shingle waited outside President Grosvenor's office. His previous meeting was running twenty minutes late. She hated to be kept waiting.

The door opened, and four, old, white men in dark suits spilled into the outer office. Their mood was dour with a hint of bourbon and entitlement. After they filed past, President Grosvenor said, "I'm sorry to have kept you waiting, Mary. Please come inside."

He didn't offer her a cigar or drink but merely motioned to the chair. "How are things going with our little project?"

"Well, it isn't working out like I had planned."

"No, it certainly has not. We are eight weeks into the semester, and it is a disaster. Have you seen today's student paper?"

"Not yet. Why?"

"There is a rather lengthy article about SMS 301. It seems Dr. Byrne has not wilted under the pressure and has, by their account, flourished."

"I'm as surprised as anyone."

"I quote, 'The class has been generating a lot of buzz and not just on Twitter and Facebook but among the student body. Last Wednesday, 145 students showed up to hear the lecture, which is impressive considering there are only 104 people enrolled in the class.' It goes on from there talking about some of the blogs the students have created. It seems one student's post on global fuel prices got picked up by CNN."

"Really, CNN?"

"Damn it! Dr. Byrne has become more than just a drunken blight on this university's sterling reputation. He has left his stain on me."

Mary didn't know where he was going with this. "I understand. I'm upset, too. I was so looking forward to being rid of him, but what can I do? We can't fire him for doing a good job."

"He isn't just doing a good job; he is becoming a goddamn hero. Yesterday, registration began. Do you know how long it took for SMS 301 to fill up?"

It was obviously a rhetorical question, so she shrugged.

"Twenty-three minutes. At 8:23 all the slots were taken. Never in the history of this school has a class been so popular," he screamed and slammed the paper down on his desk.

"I guess we underestimated him."

"I guess I underestimated you!"

"That's not fair. I've kept a close eye on him, but..."

"Do you know who those men leaving my office were?"

"No, I don't."

"They are on the search committee for a major Ivy League school, and my name has just moved from the long list to the short one."

"Congrats, so does that mean his success is helping?"

"No, that is not what it means! They are going over every detail of life here on our little college campus with only one goal: to find a reason to knock me out of the running. They are aware of Dr. Byrne and asked why I hadn't handled the situation sooner. I've explained that he is on the way out, but now I need to make that happen. Do you understand?"

"I'm not sure I do. What do you propose I do? He obviously isn't going to get the bad reviews we need to make a claim he has failed. It looks like the plan is dead."

"Mary, you are a fine administrator, but your creative thinking prowess leaves a bit to be desired. There is more than one way to skin a drunken, tenured professor."

Mary said nothing.

"If we can't get him for poor performance, what else might we have at our disposal?"

124

"I'm sure I don't know. I thought we had him at the beginning of the semester. What are you suggesting?"

"Think Mary. You know our charter and bylaws better than anyone."

Mary did think, but she was in a poor mood after all of his abuse. Nothing came to mind.

"Have you considered the morality clause?"

"I have not," she said. Her voice changed, "But you may be onto something."

He let her think. The wheels were turning, and it would be better if it was her idea.

"The morality clause is perfect. This weekend, with everyone in town for homecoming, the game, and the chances that we will win on Saturday, will make it a festive time."

"Yes, go on."

She started to pace, "While it is surprising how quickly he has adapted, he is still the same Philistine he was at the beginning of the semester. If Arthur is out drinking - and why wouldn't he be? - and with his rising popularity, then it is more than likely that he will find himself in a situation that is utterly inappropriate."

"My thinking exactly. How do we use that bit of information?"

"If someone posts pictures from the debauchery that I'm sure will ensue Saturday, then there is a very good chance we may see him involved."

"Yes, but is it really wise to leave it up to chance? I mean, we know he will be out among the students and alumni, but what if nobody happens to take a picture at the right time. What if it isn't posted?"

"I see your point."

"Louis Pasteur said, 'Fortune favors the prepared mind.'"

"I should make sure there is someone keeping an eye on him with a camera phone."

"That sounds like some excellent preparation."

"I have just the person."

"I don't need to know any of the details. Perhaps you'd like a cigar for later," he said, holding out the box of Cubans.

Mary took one, gave an understanding grin, and left. She thought as she walked out the door, "Finally, the chickens are homecoming to roost, Dr. Byrne."

Chapter Twenty-One

Arthur, walking with purpose, was flagged down by Eric, who asked, "Where have you been?"

"Is that an existential question?" he replied but didn't stop walking.

"I haven't seen you at the Pit in ages."

"I think it's been four days."

"Yeah, that's what I said."

"I've been refusing to admit I have a problem and have instead chosen to gradually cut back on my social drinking."

"How's that treating you?"

"Slow and steady, my friend, slow and steady."

"What about this weekend?"

"Homecoming? I'll be undoing all the good work I've done and then some."

"Seriously, though, what have you been up to?" "Just hanging out in the virtual worlds of social media."

"You're taking this class far more seriously than you should."

"I'm embracing the future, and you would be amazed how much stupid stuff there is to make fun of online. I've got to get to a meeting with my TAs."

Arthur entered the study room at the library. It had become the de facto meeting space because he didn't like the lighting in the normal conference room.

"Morning, everyone, let's get started. I want to begin by asking if anyone has read Susan's post she put up last night?"

Susan blushed.

"I'm assuming the silence means no. I read it this morning over breakfast and I've got to say it's fantastic. In the last few weeks your writing has gotten razor sharp. I want to highlight your post during tomorrow's class."

"What's the post about?" Kurt asked.

Arthur said, "Why don't you tell them, Susan?"

"I wrote about the battle between Apple and Samsung from the point of view of their most loyal fans."

Kurt said, "Great idea."

"Thanks."

Arthur said, "It was both thoughtful and funny. I didn't know you had that in you."

Susan shrugged.

Brian D. Meeks

Arthur continued, "I've got an idea for the mid-term paper. I think we should have everyone write about their experiences with blogging and give three pieces of advice to people who want to give it a try."

Wen asked, "How long will the paper be?"

Arthur said, "I was thinking a thousand words."

Wen asked, "Are they going to turn in their papers or post them on their blogs?"

Arthur didn't answer. He paced a little and asked, "I hadn't thought about that. What do the rest of you think?"

Lawrence said, "If we let them post on their blogs, some students may just take the ideas from their friends."

Arthur nodded then said, "Couldn't they do that anyway?"

"Yes, but it would be much easier."

A. said, "If we had them all post at the same time, say an hour before class on the day it is due, that might solve the problem."

"A., good idea," Arthur said. He asked, "Is it overkill?"

Wen answered, "It seems like almost all of the students have really gotten into blogging."

Lawrence added, "If I had a chance to do that for my mid-terms, I would have loved it. The paper feels less like an assignment and more like creating something of value."

"Susan, you have anything to add?"

"I like it," she said with a thumbs up.

"Okay, that is settled. Next, tomorrow I want to talk about building followers or, more accurately, the incredibly stupid hashtag '#TeamFollowBack.'"

A. asked, "Why is it stupid?"

"I'm glad you asked. I've been noticing when I check on some of the more prolific students on Twitter that they have built some massive follower bases."

"Isn't that good?" A. asked, looking confused.

"I believe it is a mirage. I've checked the Twitter streams of many people who have the hashtag #TeamFollowback in their bios. Most of what they are tweeting is completely self-serving. They don't, as a rule, retweet nor do they have genuine conversations. They do friend follow Friday and seem only to be interested in getting a really big follower number. What does that tell us about people who preach #TeamFollowBack?"

Kurt said, "That they're self-centered."

"Yes. Will these paragons of self-promotion become a fan of your blog?"

"I don't know. Maybe," Kurt said.

"No, they won't. They are the devil. They are chasing multi-level marketing dreams. They don't have real friends and likely only bathe when it is absolutely necessary. They don't get Twitter. #TeamFollowBack folks don't understand that the goal is to build a community by helping others and then, if one is lucky, they might have earned the respect needed for a retweet."

"That seems harsh."

"Harsh would have been to point out that these dregs of social media really were the reason their parents divorced and have likely caused global warming by exhaling C02. They should die."

Wen said, "You can't tell some of your students they should die."

Arthur gave a sigh and said, "I could, but your point is valid. I shouldn't. I'm not really thinking about our students, though. I focus my wrath on the quote-unquote social media gurus who have 50,000 fake followers."

Lawrence asked, "So, if they don't have #TeamFollow-Back in their bios does that mean they are legit?"

"Not exactly. I'd like to talk about lists and something I've found that I think is interesting. I've been checking the ratio of how many times a person is 'listed' and dividing it by the number of 'followers.' When I look at someone who I suspect is a fake, their ratio is between one to two percent. Conversely, the people whom I've gotten to know, the ones with a lot of followers but who also are willing to have discussions, have a ratio greater than five percent."

Wen asked, "So, is your point that one should be careful about who they follow?"

"Yes and, to a lesser extent, who they allow to follow them."

Kurt asked, "Why does it matter if they are following you?"

"It's simple. If I let 100 worthless people follow me, knowing that they aren't going to be engaging or help me with my goals in any way, then they are of no value and are simply ruining my listed:follower ratio."

"Yes, but why does the ratio matter if you are the only one who looks at it?" Lawrence asked.

"That is an exceptionally reasonable and logical question and will not be tolerated."

Lawrence laughed.

"In truth, it doesn't matter unless one wants to have an accurate understanding of their own social platform. If one wants to be honest with themselves and, admittedly, who really wants that, but if they did, then it is our responsibility to show the students the best way to manage their platforms."

Wen was smiling broadly and taking notes.

"Do you have something to add?"

"It seems like I just got done listening to you fight against technology. Look at you now."

"Who knew I could adapt to this century? Okay, that is all I have for today. Anyone else have something we need to discuss?"

Lawrence said, "Saturday I'm having a massive party for homecoming. You are all invited, even you, Dr. Byrne."

Arthur said, "It would be grotesquely inappropriate for me to attend such a function. Shall I bring some dip... possibly a bit of brie?"

Lawrence chuckled and said, "We're good, thanks."

Arthur said, "Okay, I think that is all. Keep up the good work."

Chapter Twenty-Two

"Yes, do come in, Tricia." Mary said.

"You wanted to see me?"

"I understand you've applied for one of the open writer positions at the student paper?"

"I think I would learn a lot from the experience," Tricia said.

"I'm sure you would. Of course, there are quite a few applicants. Just over a hundred and only three spots."

"I tried last year, too, but they hired Jackie. I have to admit she's done a good job. Her piece on the animal shelter was great."

"Tell me, why do you think you would make a good investigative journalist?"

"I'm not afraid to get my hands dirty. I worked at my high school paper and uncovered a scandal involving our librarian. I found the proof that she was skimming from the book-buying budget. It took a lot of digging, but I got her."

"I'm impressed," Mary said. She stood and looked out her office window. "Of course, high school is different than working for a college paper, especially one so fine as ours. I've read your writing sample. It was solid, but what I would like to know is how you would handle an assignment." Mary returned to her desk.

"What if you gave me one as a test? I'm sure I could win you over."

Mary smiled and said, "That is an interesting suggestion. An assignment as a test, yes, that would demonstrate your abilities. Let me think for a moment."

"I could investigate that restaurant downtown; I've heard they might be using some questionable suppliers."

"A fine idea, but I'm not sure that relates enough to campus life. What if…"

"I can do it!"

"You haven't heard my idea, but I love the enthusiasm."

"Sorry, I didn't mean to interrupt."

"I have some concerns about a professor."

"What sort of concerns?"

"I've heard rumors that he may be fraternizing with students in a way that is neither professional nor acceptable. If this is true, it is the sort of thing that would potentially damage our sterling reputation. We wouldn't want that, would we?"

"No! Who is it?"

"Dr. Arthur Byrne. Do you know him?"

There was a pause. Tricia said, "Yes, I've heard of him but never had him for a class. There was an article about him in the paper this week. He's very popular."

"Popular or not, do we want to ignore his behavior?"

"I guess not. You want me to look into it?"

"I've been told he spends a lot of time in that filthy bar Edgar's Pit. Do you know it?"

"Uhm...yes."

"Of course, we would need proof. Any accusations of immoral behavior would need to be ironclad, you understand."

Tricia said, "I'm not sure. What do you want me to do?"

"Oh, nothing like that, dear, please, I want you to be a reporter. Investigate and see if he is crossing any lines like people say. Do you have a camera on your phone?"

"Yes."

"Are you up for the challenge?"

"Sure, I guess so."

"I have every faith that you will do a remarkable job and will make an excellent reporter," Mary said, standing and escorting Tricia to the door.

Mary returned to her desk and dialed. "This is Mary. Is President Grosvenor available?"

A moment later he answered, "Mary, do you have anything interesting to report?"

"The young lady I thought might be perfect is on board."

"When do you think you'll have something?"

"It's Wednesday, so I would guess that by either Friday or Saturday she should be able to get us what we need."

"Keep me posted," he said and hung up.

"Hey, what's up?" Arthur said, putting his phone on speaker.

"I just got out of class and was thinking I might head down to the Pit. What are you up to?"

"Just tweeting, liking, and chatting on G+; you know, living the dream."

"Are you tweeting now? I can hear you typing."

"I'm able to multi-task, and yes."

Eric laughed and said, "Okay, so I just brought up Twitter. Are you having a conversation about Joseph Heller with a guinea pig?"

"We both agree that Major Major Major Major was one of best characters in the history of literary fiction. He is a very well-read guinea pig."

"I'm sure. What do you say about the Pit?"

Arthur said, "Sure, why not. Are you at your office?"

"Yes."

"Okay, I'll mosey on over to the Pit."

"Mosey?"

"I may have been tweeting with a guy from Texas earli-er."

"And he used mosey?"

"No, but I like to think he might given the chance."

"I'll order you a sarsaparilla."

Arthur hit "End" on his phone, tweeted, "Later, got to run," to the guinea pig, and gave a quick check to make sure Maltese's bowl had food.

The leaves were turning, and the campus looked post-card-worthy. Arthur, wearing a light jacket, stopped to chat with a couple of students. Somewhere along the way, he had found peace. There was still plenty of things to get his dander up, but Arthur had let go of the ghosts that had kept him miserable for the last ten years.

Eric waved from a table and said, "They didn't have a sarsaparilla, so I got you a beer."

"Thanks," Arthur said, looking around. "Where's Emi-ly?"

"She had papers to grade."

"Doesn't she have minions for that?"

"That's what I said, but she said she wanted to do it."

"What sort of crazy woman are you dating?"

"I'm not really sure about that."

"You should get her checked by a trained professional."

"Oh, not that. The dating part."

"Trouble in Ericdise?"

Eric gave a non-committal grunt and took a drink of beer.

"What's wrong, little buckaroo?"

"I miss the days when you were the grumpy, old man, and I was the optimist. Any chance of you going back to bitter?"

"There is always a chance."

"Speaking of amor."

"Were we? I was trying to steer the conversation to sex."

"Okay, sex then. What's the deal with that TA of yours?"

"Lawrence? He's really not my type."

"The hot, little Asian TA that bosses you around."

"Lou?"

"That doesn't sound right."

"Her name is Wen."

"Yes, that's her. Usually by this point in the semester you've woven your brooding spell. How about Kristen from a few years back? She was disturbingly hot."

"Nothing to tell. I guess I've been too busy."

"Too busy. That is a lame excuse. How am I supposed to live vicariously through you with that sort of attitude?"

"I think I've noticed her skirts are getting shorter the last few weeks."

"Keep your eyes off Wen's skirts."

"Ha! I knew it."

"You know nothing. She's a nice kid."

Eric took a sip of beer and said, "She's no kid. If I may quote one of the great thinkers of this century or any other, 'She's hotter than a hot tamale in hot pants on a hot plate in Hotlanta.'"

"That was one of my better quotes. She does have a nice figure."

"You disgust me with your new grown-up attitude."

Arthur laughed and said, "I'm sure it's just a phase. Emily is a bit of a knockout, too. Maybe I'll spend some time living vicariously through your wild exploits."

"I need another beer."

Chapter Twenty-Three

The weekend arrived along with the parents and alumni.

"Autumn has such a comforting smell," Arthur said as he and Emily walked along towards the stadium.

Emily asked, "Now who are we tailgating with?"

"Some of the grad students your boy-toy Eric works with. I'm sure he's wondering where we are," Arthur said.

"I'm sorry. I had to finish the potato salad. And I wouldn't call him that."

"Are you sure you don't want me to carry it for a while?"

"I'm fine but thanks."

"What was I saying? I was waxing poetic and working toward pretentious, if I recall. Oh, yes, the smell of a fine, fall football Saturday. Spring is such a girl. She gets credit for love, hope, renewal, and the dream of what might be.

Summer is all, 'Hey dude, it's warm; let's party.' It's truly the fraternity brother of the four seasons. Fall, to me, seems like the bad-ass who is about to hop on his Harley and drive off into the sunset because he's not going to listen to that bitch winter go on and on about how nobody likes her and the snow drifts make her look fat."

"I think you missed poetic, wide right, so you'll be hard pressed to make pretentious this half."

"You just watch. It will take less than two beers and a hotdog before one of those little grad students wades into the deep end of literature."

"What will you do then?"

"I will unleash a snarkstorm of pretentiousness that will blind at first then explode into a mockalanche that crushes their spirits."

"Is that why you stopped writing? Because you couldn't refrain from making up words?"

"I was severely injured when a group of grammar Nazis revoked my dictionary and thesaurus in an early morning raid. Word had spread that I was making unauthorized additions in the margins. That sort of thing is frowned upon in polite society. I was branded with a puce letter 'r.'"

"What does the 'r' stand for?"

"'Riter'...it is so shameful. Anyway, they pummeled and buffeted me about the pate, figuratively, while they spoke in tongues...tongues that always ended a sentence with a preposition. Finally, they took my brand new Moleskin and cast it asunder before mine eyes, and it was done. Telling tales with words came to me nevermore."

"That's a sad story...as in deplorably bad."

"I see they haven't come for your dictionary."

"No."

"There's Eric. I'll have to finish the rest of the story later; it's in iambic pentameter."

Emily waved with her non-potato salad holding hand.

Arthur had a burger and one beer. He listened to other people tell their stories and didn't, for possibly the first time in his life, have the uncontrollable urge to cast aspersions. He was, to use a word that few ever associated with Dr. Byrne, polite.

The grilling was being handled masterfully by Eric. Footballs were tossed about, and numerous games of baggo added to the festive air. The twelve o'clock kickoff approached. When they heard the band playing the school's fight song, a sea of red made its way to the stadium.

The first quarter saw them jump to a 7-3 lead, but a turnover just after the start of the second quarter led to a touchdown for the opponents from Down South. It was tradition not to say their arch-rival's name as it was considered profane. At the half, the team that would not be mentioned led 13 – 7. Arthur was concerned.

Eric, who sat between Arthur and Emily, said, "Our defense is doing fine, but what happened to our passing game?"

"It's like the quarterback is afraid. His timing has been terrible. How many times has he thrown the ball behind a wide-open man?"

"Six."

"Exactly! He couldn't complete a pass in a sobriety-free sorority."

Emily leaned forward and said, "Okay, that was clever. Much better than before."

Eric asked, "Before?"

"Yes. On the walk over he was trying to make up a story. It was dreadful."

Arthur said, "It was only dreadful because you didn't appreciate the nuance of my genius."

Eric shook his head and patted Emily on the knee. "I'm sorry you had to endure that."

Arthur said, "Thank you. It was nearly unbearable having such a remarkable bit of off the cuff storytelling fall on blonde ears."

Emily said, "First off, I'm a brunette..."

"You're a metaphorical blonde."

Emily lost her train of thought and let a giggle slip. "Okay, 'metaphorical blonde.' That was pretty good."

Arthur got up and said, "I'm off for beer. It's my turn to buy." He needed to get away from third wheeldom.

A few former students stopped to chat. One introduced her husband who seemed like a nice fellow. Arthur made small talk but was thinking about the late-night tutoring he had provided during her senior year. She was an eager student and interested in literature. Ah, good times.

He missed the second-half kickoff and the 98-yard return for a touchdown. Three minutes later, Arthur nearly spilled his beer when the redshirt freshman corner intercepted a tipped ball and took it to the house.

The team from Down South fell apart after that. The final score was 35 – 13. Arthur, who had been caught up in the game, didn't notice that wheels one and two had gotten somewhat icy towards one another.

He bid them adieu in a really bad French accent and went home to take a nap. Seeing Kimberly or Kristen - or was it Crystal? - had put him in a mood to celebrate the win, but a post-game, pre-Lawrence-party battery recharge was needed.

Chapter Twenty-Four

Arthur put on some sweats and almost climbed into bed for a post-game nap. He instead went out and looked at his typewriter with the one word "Monday" that had been trying to get him to write all semester. He pulled the page out and set it aside.

On a fresh sheet he typed, "She was a metaphorical blonde, but she was also much more than most people could see."

The buzz from the tailgating hadn't worn off. He didn't like the first line. It was okay, though; he would fix it later. His fingers pounded the typewriter with reckless abandon. Maltese hopped up on the table and laid down to watch Arthur work. Eventually, Maltese decided it wasn't very exciting and drifted off, flicking his tail whenever Arthur yanked a page out of the carriage.

Arthur had no idea where he was going with the story. Each paragraph seemed to give a clue as to what was next. A thought would become words and they would lead him down the path. He wasn't writing to impress; he was just writing.

His phone rang from underneath the cat. Maltese didn't appreciate it at all and left to find a better spot for slumber. "Hey, Wen, what's up?"

"Did you go to the game?"

"I did. It was awesome. I'm writing. I've got to go."

"Really? Are you coming to Lawrence's party?"

"Maybe. Call me later," he said and hung up.

Without so much as a pause he started right back up. He could see it all in his beer-addled mind. It only needed to be written down. Arthur was like a court reporter. He hoped the story would continue to be interesting.

The phone rang again. Arthur answered, "Eric, I'm writing. Call me later."

"I know. Wen just..."

Arthur ended the call. His characters had left the restaurant and were getting on a trolley, which was surprising since Arthur had no idea they were in San Francisco until that moment. He decided they needed heavier clothing. The detail made him stop because there hadn't been any discussion about what they were wearing. Arthur started to obsess about hats.

He stopped and stood up. Arthur really wanted the woman to be wearing a bowler. "The Woman in the Bowler Hat" struck him as a good title. Why would she be wearing such a hat, though? It didn't make sense. He had almost written himself into a corner. Maybe a nice knit hat would be cute?

The man had a baseball hat on. It fit snugly and kept his head warm, but she was there, in his mind, wearing that bowler. It looked really cute on her, but it just didn't make any sense. Maybe she was an actress? Arthur asked. She wasn't.

It occurred to him that he was making an assumption. Arthur didn't know of any women who wore bowler hats, but that didn't mean it wasn't possible. His computer would know. In the Google search bar he typed "women in bowler hats."

It turned out some women did wear them. He sat back down, put a hat on her head, and continued on. It didn't stop - the words, the story, the images in his mind. It was a rush. Arthur needed to eat, but he didn't want to quit writing.

It was starting to get hard to see the paper. When he turned on the light, he found Maltese back on the table. Maltese meowed.

"Are you hungry?"

Maltese jumped to the floor and ran to his bowl.

148

Arthur made a turkey sandwich. He ate it and watched the cat. Now, he needed a nap.

Arthur eased out of his nap and laid in bed enjoying the warmth of the covers. The digital clock read 9:17, but there was an implied, "So, why not just stay in bed and sleep until morning?" Eight minutes of watching the clock later, his phone rang. He didn't recognize the number and answered in a drowsier voice than normal.

"Yeah, this is Arthur."

"Hey, it's Crystal."

Interesting. Maybe her name really was Crystal, but I better be cautious. "Sorry, I was in a dead sleep and wasn't really listening. Who?"

"Crystal. We ran into you at the game."

"Oh, yes, I met your husband. We got to chatting and missed the opening kickoff of the second half, but it was worth it to see you again."

"I hear there is a great party going on at 'The Hill.' You still like to do shots and talk literature?"

"I do. Believe it or not, I've actually started to write again."

"No way! You never told me why you stopped. What is it about?"

"It's too early to tell, but the beginning doesn't suck."

149

"I can't wait to hear all about it."

"I'm not sure your husband would enjoy some old ex... professor of yours...going on about his scribbling."

"That's okay. He's staying in and working. It is so dull. I'll be all by my lonesome."

"Such a horrible atrocity just waiting to happen."

"You'll make an appearance?"

"I'll be there with airs of superiority on."

"Ciao."

Arthur threw off the warm comforter and showered. As he was shaving, Maltese seemed to be curious as to what was going on. "Yes, I'm shaving at night. I'll grant you it is unusual, but Arthur is going out..."

Maltese meowed.

"You're right. I shall not speak of myself in the third person again. I hate that. Anyway, there's a soiree that promises to offer plenty of opportunities for self-aggrandizing displays of literary snobbery."

Maltese laid down in the doorway.

"The long and short of it is that nubile women of an inappropriate age and questionable intelligence will find themselves overwhelmingly interested in demonstrating their prowess in all sorts of unspeakable hidden talents."

Maltese stretched and rolled onto his back.

"As an educator, though it clearly goes against a societal norm of what is proper and it pains me so, I'm willing to endure the hushed tones of disapproval to allow for their personal growth. It's quite big of me, really."

Maltese grew bored and left.

Arthur got dressed and was tying his shoes when the phone rang. "Hello, Lou. Sorry I was so short earlier."

"No problemo, Artie."

"You've been drinking, haven't you?"

"Yes, how'd you know?"

"You've begun to channel Fonzie...and you called me Artie."

"Who? The bear?"

"That's Fozzie. Never mind."

"The party is rocking. I want to hear about this writing stuff."

"I've not gotten very far, but I'll tell you all about it when I get there...providing you haven't passed out."

"Oh, I'm just getting started. We won! Woot..."

Arthur hung up as it was apparent that the hollering might continue for some time. He changed the sheets on his bed and straightened up a bit and then left.

Lawrence's place was only a few blocks away and he could hear the revelry long before he arrived. There were people on the lawn and out back and several on the roof over the porch. A few students cheered when he arrived. He saw Lawrence wave from the porch just as Eric called.

"Where are you? I just got here."

"I think I'm going to stay in tonight," Eric said.

"What the hell?"

"Emily and I had a fight. I think it's over."

"I'm sorry. What happened?" Arthur said while greeting enthusiastic partiers.

"I don't know, but things have been a little rough and finally I couldn't take it anymore."

"So you dumped her?"

"Yes."

"Well, then why are you staying home? You should be out celebrating your newfound freedom."

"I suppose, but I just don't feel like it."

"Are you sure you're doing okay? She was nice looking...and smart."

"Don't rub it in."

"If you can't count on your friends to kick you when you're down who can you count on?"

Arthur thought he heard a smile in the goodbye.

A curly-haired young man sporting an unimaginable amount of tie-dye made a hand gesture that seemed friendly and said, "Dude, it's Prof Byrne. Hey, Prof, did you see my blog post?"

"I'm not sure. The enthusiasm has exceeded my wildest expectations. Last week alone there were over 350 posts from class blogs. Which one are you talking about?"

"I wrote 500 words about how herb could solve global warming."

Brian D. Meeks

"I think I would have remembered that one. Send me a DM with the link. I want to check it out."

"Awesome," he said, repeating the hand gesture.

On the porch, Lawrence was waiting with a red plastic cup. "Dr. Byrne, you look parched."

Arthur smacked his lips and said, "You know what? I do feel that I may be on the cusp of a severe case of dehydration. Do you have any flat tap-water?"

"I have beer."

"I think there's water in beer, but we may want to consult someone outside the liberal arts college on that one."

Lawrence laughed and said, "I'll ask around. Hey, I hear you are writing?"

"It's true, but where did you hear that?"

"I'm not saying as I wouldn't want to incriminate my tiny Asian sister."

Arthur grinned and asked, "How is Lou? I talked with her a few minutes ago. It sounded like she had been hitting it pretty hard."

"I think she's on her second beer."

"Really?"

"Of course, she doesn't weigh more than about a buck-o-five. I'll keep an eye on her. That skirt she's wearing could be trouble."

"Good man. We've got to watch each others' backs."

"And some of their fronts," Lawrence said with a wink.

153

Arthur looked up to see who Lawrence meant. Emily and a friend were strolling towards them. She did not look like she was grieving the loss of her "in a relationship" status. He wondered if she had already updated Facebook.

The proper bro protocol would be a cold shoulder followed by overt disdain. Arthur considered it, but thought he could do better. "Hello, Emily. Who is your extraordinarily fetching friend?"

"This is Amy."

Amy extended her hand and said, "It is very nice to meet you...again."

"Ah, I am such a cad. I'm sorry I don't remember."

"Oh, no, it's nothing like that. I came to your book signing in Brooklyn. Your talk was fantastic, but that was a long time ago. I wouldn't expect you to remember."

"I remember the signing or more specifically the donuts. Most book stores avoid providing sticky things for their authors to nibble on, but they were on the cutting edge of signing technology and provided wet naps, too."

Amy laughed.

Emily smiled and said, "Yes, poor Arthur here hasn't written since then, and he won't talk about it. He's very secretive."

Amy said, "Maybe it's personal."

Arthur said, "That's not true at all. I spent several hours banging away today after the game."

Emily said, "You're teasing me."

Arthur handed his glass back to Lawrence, who was still manning the keg, and said, "Another round of your finest mead."

"One beer coming up."

Amy asked, "What are you working on? Or do you not like to talk about something before it is done?"

Emily said, "Oh, he's just teasing. He hasn't written anything in over a decade. It is a legendary and tragic case of writer's block."

Arthur could tell that Emily had been knocked off her game by his comment. He affixed his best pensive face, turned to Amy, and said, "I'm honestly not sure where it is going yet. New projects are often like that. I've a couple of characters and am exploring their afternoon. Without even intending to do so, I've started channeling my inner Faulkner and woven in stream of consciousness. It is not my usual fare, but we can't grow if we don't push the boundaries. Wouldn't you agree?"

Arthur wasn't listening to Amy's answer. He didn't care. Emily was too polite to interrupt her friend, and it appeared to be killing her. Arthur nodded at points that seemed to appropriately convey a sense of deep interest in the speaker, but he was really watching Emily and trying to process what had just happened.

The storyteller's mind, though dusty and unused for many years, was humming along pretty well considering.

Arthur could see Emily had created a narrative where she was the one to get the author through the personal hell he had created and would help him achieve his former glory. Emily, the character, had a delightful internal dialogue going on that he wished he could write down, but it would have to wait. Amy seemed to be winding down. Arthur tuned into her big finish.

"...and that is why I think As I Lay Dying is such a brilliant work," Amy said.

Before Emily could jump in, Arthur said, "I'm mostly an arrogant sod who likes to listen to himself talk and, as such, rarely give credence to anyone's opinion, but you have nailed the essence of Faulkner."

Amy seemed to be at a loss for words.

The high praise found its mark. Emily looked to be reeling. Arthur thought she was going to go down, but Lawrence stepped in. The round was over; the bell had sounded.

"What can I get you ladies? We've got beer, obviously, and quite a lot of wine inside. If you're thinking something harder, well, we've got that, too. The bartender by the tiki torches can hook you up."

Amy asked for a beer, still glowing, as Emily thanked Lawrence, but Arthur didn't hang around. He used their moment of distraction to slip into the house.

Once inside, Arthur found himself partnered with the friend of one of his students for a match of beer pong. It took little time for a crowd to gather; it seemed Arthur was a fan favorite. It wasn't enough, and he and his bubbly teammate were bounced.

Arthur didn't mind as the next team had been sitting on a couch, and their seat was now empty. He settled into it. He seemed to have found a fine spot. The song changed from a formulaic beat with a lot of bass to "Sympathy for The Devil".

"You made it," Wen said.

"Lou?"

"What do you think?"

The pirouette lasted just long enough for Arthur to wipe the gawk from his face.

"On a scale of one to 'I don't think your mother would approve,' I'd say 'wow.'"

"Thanks," she said and introduced her two friends. "This is Fiona and Cheryl."

"Where's Bosley?"

Fiona and Wen laughed, but Cheryl didn't get the joke.

Wen flopped down on Arthur's right and Fiona on his left. Cheryl grabbed a corner of the coffee table and said, "Wen says you're a famous author."

"Have you ever heard of me?"

"No."

"Then I'm obviously not."

"You're not an author?" Cheryl asked, seeming confused.

"No, I am, but if you've never heard of me then I must not be famous."

Fiona said, "I've heard of you."

Wen leaned her shoulder into Arthur's and said, "I want to hear about your new book."

Arthur didn't answer at first as he was momentarily struck dumb by Wen's expertly executed leg cross. He could tell it wasn't her first leg cross, either. Arthur found it strangely enticing and disturbing. "Well, I can't say for sure that it will end up a book, but it was a pretty good start."

It wasn't Arthur's first time, either. He may not have known where his writing was heading, but he knew how to tell a story, and he wove a beauty. A little bit about the characters to start whetted their appetites. Fiona jumped in with a question, which led to an heroic explanation. Three hot women, gathered in rapt adoration, had a gravitational pull that defies Newtonian physics...and Newtonian physicists. Two frat boys, who didn't realize they were being drawn into a talk about writing, pulled up chairs.

In the world of self-aggrandizement, a smart move was to circle back from time to time so that the new folks could be brought up to speed. It needed to be handled with a deft touch, but there were a few tricks one could learn, and Arthur had invented most of them. He took the last pull of his beer and held the cup upside down.

With a sad look deep into Cheryl's eyes he said, "It pains me to see such a fine cup empty. Oh, well, where was I?"

"If you promise not to continue without me...and to save my spot, I'll grab you another beer."

Channeling P.T. Barnum, Arthur said, "Ladies and gentlemen, a round of applause for Cheryl who is willing to right a terrible wrong."

The crowd, now close to a dozen, cheered.

Fiona said, "Hey, would you take our picture?" She handed her phone to the frat guy who had been checking her out.

Fiona and Wen snuggled up close and smiled. Arthur was already smiling.

"Let me see," Arthur asked.

Fiona showed him and Wen. This led to a picture with Wen's phone and an even tighter Arthur sandwich.

Arthur heard a few mumblings about why the crowd was gathering, and he seized the moment. "Oh, I was just answering Wen's question about my new book. Do you like to read?'

Most wouldn't admit they didn't, so it was a safe question. After the "yes," Arthur gave a quick recap of all the crowd had missed.

The crowd was enthralled. Arthur used fine brush strokes to paint his story. Had Cheryl returned with only the beer, he might have continued on until he had a fresco that rivaled the Sistine Chapel's. She had, in fact, come back with Arthur's beer, which she only promised to give him if he did a Jell-O shot.

The cookie sheet full of Jell-O shots looked ominous to Arthur. The crowd cheered. Wen said, "I bet this is how Bill Cosby gets drunk," and handed one to Fiona.

Cheryl took one and passed the tray off to someone else as she handed Arthur his beer.

Fiona said, "To Cosby," and raised her shot.

Arthur raised his and added, "Why is there air?" He tilted his head back. The shot was grape Jell-O and vodka. It was so good that he didn't care if anyone got his reference. It wouldn't be their last shot.

Chapter Twenty-Five

Sleep ceased, but he wasn't ready to give up. His eyes remained shut. His only thought was I'm awake; now what? Arthur bounced the query off the inside of his head. It echoed, but nobody answered. Again he asked, but only silence. A third attempt and subsequent failure made him think he might be dead, but that was a thought and a start.

Arthur's eyes barely opened. A familiar ceiling greeted and comforted him. He reached a conclusion: he wasn't dead. In an unrelated bit of thinking, Arthur decided he might like a painting above his bed that gave the illusion of a Gothic dome. The idea kept him occupied for a while.

Thirst was a problem, but Arthur couldn't work out how to get a straw strong enough or of sufficient length to make it from his bed to the refrigerator. He considered the difficulty in opening the door, removing the water pitcher, and filling the glass. Maybe it was a magic straw that could go through the door straight into the water. Regardless, he didn't have such a straw.

He closed his eyes again, defeated.

More than water, Arthur wanted to return to that place where dreams happened because they likely had water or, at the very least, the straw of Zeus. It had to be the sort of thing the gods used on Mount Olympus after a night of too many ambrosia shots.

He could not return, but there wasn't any reason he needed to open his eyes. Nope, he wouldn't do it. Nobody could make him.

A voice stirred and said, Too bad you weren't more strong-willed last night.

Arthur wasn't sure where his little voice was going with this.

You seemed to be made to drink by everyone.

Arthur knew the mountain of evidence bore this out. He could hear a streetcar named "hangover" coming down the street. It wouldn't be long now.

The start of the Jell-O shots was the last saved memory that remained uncorrupted on his brain. He could recall an eloquent proclamation that "Jell-O was to be brought forth for all in the kingdom." There wasn't any indication who the speaker might have been, but the voice sounded eerily Arthur-like.

162

Had Crystal delivered round two?

His mental camera must have gone out at that point because there was a long period of black. The audio said something about "body shots." The voice might have been Emily's or Amy's, but he wasn't sure. The crowd's cheers were clear, though.

The audio track died out, too.

The next memory was from Edgar's Pit. It made little sense, but a discussion seemed to have centered around the rules for a pants exchange. This seemed like it might be a "bad" memory.

Without opening his eyes, Arthur did a check. He was not wearing pants or anything else for that matter. This realization caused a flash of understanding.

People had been in his home; not a lot but a smattering. He couldn't give a count, but he was confident at least one of them, female, had been sans pants as well.

With only the slightest of head turns managed, he peeked out from under his eyelids to find the other half of the bed empty. His ears, which had started to ring a bit, listened for sounds from deep in the abode. Nothing.

It seemed safe to open his eyes further.

The light on the ceiling seemed to be lying to him. It was morning light. Arthur knew morning light because he had looked upon it with such scorn many times. It couldn't be Sunday morning light, could it?

Maybe I've slept clean through to Monday?

163

The thought cheered him some. Not that he needed it. He was starting to come to the realization that he had been through some serious adult fun. No amount of hangover could take that from him. He took some deep breaths.

If one word were to be used, he might choose amazing. No, that was far too pedestrian. How about fantastic? It didn't do the justice that was due. He could only describe her in one way: enthusiastic.

The next realization cleared away the fog. He COULD only describe her in one way. Another way, say...her name...that didn't seem to be an option.

Fuck!

Arthur sat up, swung his feet out of bed, and, with trepidation, stood. His legs did an admirable job of taking him to the bathroom.

The shower was fantastic. A few more memories came back. It looked like the hangover was going to be more manageable than he first thought. By the time he reached the rinse cycle, his brain reminded him of his new writing project.

This made him happier than the fragmented bits of sex memory. Still, he was curious.

When he got out of the shower, he saw that the steamed mirror had a heart and read "XOXO ~"

Arthur put writing thoughts aside. He knew what an "X" meant and an "O," but the tilde had him stumped. A

164

quick run through of possible candidates who might have penned this steamy note left him with a list of three. He couldn't narrow it further.

In the kitchen he grabbed after a tall glass of water. Arthur noticed the cat bowls had some food and water. His guest had fed Maltese. Two points for the mystery woman.

A garbage bag full of bottles and cans was next to the back door. She had collected the dead soldiers, too. Another point for her. He took in his abode in its entirety. It was clean...too clean.

There wasn't any sign of debauchery to be had. Not a clue as to what had transpired anywhere. The crime scene had been scrubbed.

Arthur removed two points from the mystery woman's score card and went to find Maltese. The cat was resting on the back of the couch. He looked to be considering a nap and couldn't be bothered with a proper greeting. All Arthur got was a slight tail flick.

The Underwood sat ready. Arthur's work-in-progress remained where he had left it. It was a new day, and he was going to write.

Chapter Twenty-Six

Tricia didn't recognize the number but answered anyway. "Hello?"

"Good morning. I hope I didn't wake you."

"No, that's okay."

"I was just checking in to see how your article was coming."

"Actually, I have an even better idea for an article. You won't believe it. Dr. Arthur Byrne announced last night that he began a new novel. It was amazing. After over a decade with nothing, this is such huge news. I did some research last night after I got home, and he still has a sizable fan base that has been wondering if he would ever write again. It is the sort of story that could go national."

There was a long silence. Mary said, "That is interesting, but his days of contributing to the literary world are past. I doubt he could piece together a decent 'See Jane

Run' let alone anything noteworthy. I'm going to need you to stick with our original story idea. I'd like to see the copy this afternoon. Did you get the photos?"

"Well, yes, but I think..."

"Please send them over and I'll take a look. Now, I'd better let you get back to writing."

Kurt walked into the conference room and said, "Has anyone else read..."

Everyone had the paper in front of them.

Lawrence said, "This can't be good."

Kurt asked, "Has anyone talked with Dr. Byrne yet?"

A. said, "Wen and I have both called, but he hasn't picked up. I think his phone is off."

Kurt sat down next to Wen who gave him a half-smile. Everyone went back to their papers. Kurt gave Wen a little nudge en lieu of a "how you doing?" She just shrugged and looked down at her phone.

Ten minutes passed. Lawrence's phone buzzed. He read it aloud. "It's from Dr. Byrne. 'I can't make it today. Sorry. Lawrence, you'll teach the lecture this week.'"

Wen said, "I've got to go," and left.

There was silence for a few seconds. Kurt said, "I'm going, too. I'll call you later, Lawrence."

Kurt caught up with Wen outside of the library. She wasn't moving very quickly. "Are you all right?"

"I know the girl in the picture or one of them at least."

"Which one?"

"The one in the pink bra sitting on his lap and sucking his neck."

"Who is she?"

"She's my friend Cheryl. She, Fiona, and I went to the party together."

"That's Cheryl? You introduced us at Lawrence's place, but I didn't recognize her. Have you talked to her yet?"

"Yeah, she's pretty upset, but at least you can't really see her face."

"Who's the other woman?"

"No idea, but I think she used to be a TA for Dr. Byrne."

"This looks pretty bad."

Wen started to cry. "It's my fault. All of it."

"Girl, what are you talking about?"

"At the party, Fiona, Cheryl, and I got him hammered."

"He doesn't need any help. I saw him. He was pretty out of control."

"I know, but if we hadn't started doing the jello shots. I mean, that picture is bad, but..." Wen showed him some pictures on her phone as she wiped her eyes. They sat down at one of the secluded benches next to the founder's statue.

Kurt started to flip through the pictures. He said, "Did I tell you how much I liked your outfit?"

"Thanks."

"I love your top...Oh, wait, no top in this one...where is this at?"

"After the Pit, Fiona and two of her friends, who we ran into at the bar, and I all went back to Dr. Byrne's place."

"Oh, I missed the after hours."

"It got a little out of hand."

"More out of hand than, well, the rest of the evening?"

"I don't drink that often. Sometimes my clothes fall off when I do."

Kurt laughed and said, "I knew there was a saucy side to you."

"You have no idea."

"Keep going. What happened?"

"Fiona made margaritas and spilled something on her top, so she took it off. Her friend screamed something, and, before I knew it, everyone was mostly in their underwear."

"What about Dr. Byrne?"

"He was shirtless and singing Jimmy Buffett."

"Can he sing?"

"He can sing Jimmy Buffett that's for sure."

"So?"

"Eventually even Fiona passed out, and I'm not going to lie...I..."

"You didn't?"

"More than once."

"You little tramp."

"I really am."

"How was it?"

"I'm not going to give you all the sordid details, but it worked out just like I had hoped. That is why it is all my fault. I went to that party to throw myself at Arthur. Now look at what's happened."

Kurt put his arm around her, "It's okay. I'm sure it will all be over in a day or two."

"Yes, but why won't he answer his phone?"

"Let's go see him. You can give me some more details on the way. I'm going to need you to dish everything, you little tramp."

Wen smiled and looped her arm through Kurt's.

The walk across campus wasn't easy. It seemed everyone had the paper open to the same story. Two guys with skateboards were giving each other high-fives while another group of six were laughing and making jokes.

When they got to the house, all the shades were drawn. His car was out front, so they rang the bell. Kurt could hear Maltese scratching at the door but nothing else. He tried to look in the window but didn't see anything.

Wen knocked and said, "Arthur, are you in there?"

Kurt said, "Try again."

Knocking a little harder this time, she said, "I'm here with Kurt."

Kurt said, "Maybe he's not home. He does walk a lot."

"Yeah, I suppose. I'm worried, though."

"Me, too."

Chapter Twenty-Seven

It had been quiet for a while. Arthur had unplugged the phone then asked Google how to turn off his iPhone. He recognized the footfalls on the porch. At the sound of the knocking he said, "Come on in, Eric."

"How you doing, buddy?"

"I'm lying in a proverbial bed of my own making."

"How is it?"

"Lumpier than one might imagine."

"I brought a bottle of those Napa grapes you like so much."

Arthur started to get up.

Eric raised a hand and said, "I know where the corkscrew is. So, any reaction from Mary?"

"I have a meeting in her office tomorrow to discuss the 'situation.' I'm thinking it may be prudent to call my attorney."

"Who's the girl on your lap in the picture?"

"That's Cheryl. She's one of Lou's friends."

"What happened to her shirt?"

"I don't even remember when that was taken."

"Did you drag her home?"

"There we're in sort of a gray area."

"What do you mean?"

"Did I have an overnight guest? Yes, but it gets a little foggy at that point."

"That is awesome," Eric said, holding his glass up.

"It used to be. Somewhere along the way it became pathetic. I've been sitting here all day thinking. I can't remember when I became the guy in the picture."

"What do you mean?"

"The old geezer fondling women?"

"It looks mutual."

"It was, but that doesn't make it any better. I've become something ugly and pathetic. The thing is it has been my life for the last ten years. This semester, however, has been different. I've enjoyed teaching for the first time. It wasn't just the end-of-the-road job that kept me in single malt."

"You have seemed happy if you don't mind me using that word."

"In the past I might have, but you're right: I've found happiness isn't such a bad thing," Arthur said and set the glass of wine, untouched, down.

"This isn't the end of the world."

"The world doesn't even notice the foibles of a bitter, old man. This isn't the end of anything, but, well, me."

Eric looked concerned.

"It didn't sound so ominous in my head. What I mean is that I had found the 'me' that hadn't existed in a long time."

"Emily asked me why you stopped writing. I told her I didn't know. She got pissed. Why did you stop writing?"

"The funny thing is that I've been thinking about that most of the day. A lot of the details are gone. I remember her name, though."

"I figured it was a woman."

"What else is there?"

"So, what happened?"

"We met at a bookstore. That part is still as clear as if it had just happened. She had short, black, somewhat unkempt hair and was browsing through a book about I.M. Pei. It was fashion week in New York. She was not fashionable. Her raging indifference was intoxicating.

"I can't remember the year. I'm not sure it matters. I was young...ish, and she was life. We left the bookstore and went to a coffee house. I played the author card early. She said she knew who I was but hadn't enjoyed my last book, so she didn't want to bring it up. I was hooked.

"She wasn't, though, and it took me six months to finally wear her down. During that time, I was writing

174

more and better than I had ever done before. I wrote the Vanity Fair piece in something like forty minutes.

"Eventually, she caved and agreed to date me. She said something to the effect, 'Okay, we can date but know that it is entirely out of a sense of charity on my part.' I agreed. It was heaven.

"Sure, it sounds like cliché, and, really, those years were an unapologetic cliché, but we did it well. There were dinner parties, evenings at the theatre, art gallery openings, and, of course, the book stuff."

"What happened?"

"She dumped me."

"Why?"

"She liked kids and thought making a few seemed like a reasonable thing to consider. I thought it was an idea worthy of contempt. I mean, seriously, what sort of sick psychopath intentionally ruins their lives with offspring?"

"Did you call her a psychopath?"

"No, I used more hurtful language."

"You know, some people have children and like them."

"Where did you hear that? The internet? You know people lie on the internet."

"You don't like the wine?"

"I'm sure it's fine. I'm just not feeling it, I guess."

"So she left, and you got writer's block?"

"Something like that, but it was more a case of disinterest. I just didn't want to write; that is, until Saturday."

"You started writing again?"

"I did after the game. It isn't bad, either."

Eric asked, "Why didn't you tell me?"

"I was going to, but we started talking about you and Emily. How are you doing?"

"Eh, I'll survive. Do you think Mary is going to try to use this to fire you?"

"I imagine that's the plan."

"We can fight this."

"I'm not sure it is a good idea for you to get involved. I don't think you should let the stench of this mess rub off on you."

"I'm not afraid of Mary."

"You're still relatively young. Picking battles is something I never learned to do. If you don't learn how, you'll be me in a decade and a half."

Maltese wandered out from behind the plant in the corner and hopped onto Eric's lap. There didn't seem to be much more to say. A comfortable silence ensued.

The stillness was broken by a knock at the door.

"Come in," Arthur said.

Wen walked in and said, "You didn't answer earlier. I was worried."

"Yes, I was sulking. I'm better now. Glass of wine?"

"No, thanks."

Eric chased Maltese off his lap and said, "I've got to get going. I just wanted to check on you. Hang in there, buddy."

"Thanks for coming over. I'll talk with you later."

Arthur waited until Eric was well off the porch. "Don't look so worried. I'll be fine."

"I'm really sorry."

"For what?"

"Getting you drunk."

Arthur was still unsure of who had spent the night. He hoped it was Wen. He said, "I don't recall putting up much of a fight."

"You were outnumbered. You didn't stand a chance."

"I'll admit that had I wanted to put up a fight I'm sure it wouldn't have lasted very long. I'm powerless against a short skirt."

Wen blushed a little and sat down next to him on the couch. "I wore that skirt because I was determined to have my way with you. I didn't know it would lead to this."

"So you regret what happened?"

"No, you were great. I just mean...what if you lose your job?"

Arthur had his answer. He put his arm around her shoulder and pulled her close. He wanted to say something clever but nothing came to mind. The reassuring hug would have to do until he had a plan.

Chapter Twenty-Eight

Arthur propped himself up in bed. Wen, wearing lacy boy shorts, flipped through his dress shirts. "What are you doing?"

She pulled a peach button-down off its hanger and put it on. "What do you think?"

"Sexy as hell."

"What are you going to wear to the meeting?"

"I'm not up on current fashion. Can one wear white to an inquisition after May?"

"No. I think you should wear a suit."

"I was thinking something less formal, maybe a kilt."

"You will wear something respectful. Now, out of bed and into the shower."

Arthur crawled out of bed and grabbed Wen around her waist. He kissed her on the neck. "I think a shower sounds like a great idea."

Arthur, in his best suit, was mentally ready to take his medicine. It would be brutal, but, for the first time in years, he had something worth fighting for.

Mary opened her office door and said, "Please come in, Dr. Byrne."

Arthur, without saying a word, took the seat in front of her desk.

"I have to begin by saying how disappointed I am in your behavior. You've shown very poor judgment and left the department and the entire school with a black eye. Cavorting with women half your age, drinking and getting drunk, and showing off for the cameras like you were some twenty-year-old fraternity boy - well, it's disgraceful."

Arthur kept his retort to himself.

"Why don't you grow up? Parents send their children to our campus to sharpen their minds and prepare them for long productive lives. They do not send them here to be fondled by faculty! What have you got to say for yourself?"

"You're right; I used poor judgment."

Mary looked as though that wasn't an answer she had prepared for but continued with her lecture. It went on for over five minutes. Arthur tuned her out. Eventually, she got to the part he had been expecting.

"Until the hearing two weeks from today you will be on paid leave."

Arthur said, "I understand. Two weeks paid vacation until you decide what to do with me. Got it. Thanks for your time."

Mary sneered.

Arthur couldn't enjoy his little jab because some sort of commotion was going on outside and was getting louder. He went to the window and saw that a small group of women with signs had formed outside. It took him a moment, but he realized they were there protesting him. Words like "misogynist" and "creep" were being bandied about.

Mary looked out and said, "It seems not every one of the ladies on campus has been fooled by your charm."

Arthur left.

* * *

The building had more than one exit, and Arthur was able to avoid the picketers. He took the long way home to avoid being seen. Arthur, not known for humility, was embarrassed. He was sure Mary had put them up to it, but even so, organized group hatred wasn't something he had ever known.

Arthur got to his front porch just as the local news van pulled up. He walked in and found Wen, still wearing his shirt. He said, "I think things have taken a turn for the worse."

"What happened?"

"There was an angry mob of women protesting me, and it seems the local news has gotten whiff of the story. You best get dressed and maybe head out the back. I've got a bad feeling about this."

"I'm not going anywhere."

"Don't you have a class to get to?"

"Oh, well, actually, yes."

"I'm just saying, you might as well get out before it gets too crazy."

Wen peered through the blinds. "A second van just arrived."

"You don't have much time. If you want to be the crazy professor's mistress and get splashed all over the airwaves, there will be plenty of time for that later. For now, I'd appreciate it if I didn't have to worry about you."

Wen smiled and said, "That's sort of sweet of you."

Arthur grabbed her and said, "You look sexy as hell in my shirt, and I could spend the next two weeks curled up here with you, but I need you to go. If you head through the back yard, there is a hole in the fence. You can get away without being seen."

Wen pulled on her jeans and said, "Okay, I'll go." She put on her shoes then gave him a kiss before she left.

Arthur watched until she was gone.

It took five minutes to fill his bag with clothes. He took the bag out the back, set it in the alley, and went back inside. Arthur filled Maltese's bowls and called Eric. "I need you to do me a favor."

"Sure, anything."

"Can you feed Maltese for me?"

"Why?"

"I've been suspended, and there's something I need to do."

"When will you be back?"

"A couple of weeks. Will you look after Maltese?"

"No problem."

"Thanks."

Arthur hung up. He changed out of his suit and put on jeans and a golf shirt. He gave Maltese a pat on the head and said, "Eric is going to look after you for a little while. You're a good cat."

A third van had arrived while he packed. Arthur walked down the steps, but only one of the reporters was ready with questions. He smiled, got in his car, and drove away before anyone could get any video of his escape. He zipped around the block, picked up his bag from the alley, and left town. If the world was going to come crashing down around him so be it, but he wasn't going to be held captive in his house as it happened.

Chapter Twenty-Nine

The small group of media hounds were bored. Rebecca, a rookie journalist, hadn't been in the game long enough to become jaded. Her phone rang. She said, "Hey, boss, nothing yet."

"You think we'll have anything for tomorrow's paper?"

Rebecca walked down the street for a little privacy. "I got a hold of the woman in the picture. She's meeting me at three."

"The one in the pink bra?"

"No, the other one. The one sitting on his lap is Cheryl, but she isn't talking."

"This whole thing seems like a dog that won't hunt but go ahead."

Rebecca hung up. She looked back at the huddled mass of people waiting for Arthur to return. They were mostly

183

local television except there were two other print media people and her.

She had promised Crystal there wouldn't be any pictures, so her photographer, Stan, could keep an eye on the house. Rebecca pulled him aside and whispered, "I'm going to go meet Crystal. Here's my digital recorder in case Dr. Byrne comes back. Don't tell anyone where I'm going."

Stan had been in the business for close to twenty years, and she could tell he found her tiresome. He had made it clear he thought the whole cloak and dagger thing was stupid. "Sure, whatever. Have fun."

Rebecca took the car. It was about thirty miles to Springville, and she would need a little time to find the coffee shop.

Three o'clock came and went. Rebecca started to get annoyed by a quarter past. At 3:20, Crystal, wearing dark glasses, walked into the coffee shop. She set her jacket on the chair across from Rebecca and said, "I'm sorry I'm late. Let me grab something, and we can talk."

Rebecca got out her notebook. She hated to be kept waiting.

Crystal sat down, took off her glasses, and said, "I'm not sure what you want to talk to me about."

"I want to know about the picture."

"It's just me sitting next to Arthur at Edgar's Pit."

"Who is the woman on his lap?"

184

"I honestly don't know. She was drunk and hopped on his lap just before the picture was taken."

"Where was her shirt?"

"No idea."

"How do you know Dr. Byrne?"

There was a hesitation. Crystal took a sip of her coffee and said, "I was his teaching assistant a couple of years ago."

"What was he like to work for?"

"He was fine. He knows his stuff. Frankly, I don't see what all the fuss is about. He was just having a beer, and this crazy woman threw herself at him just before the picture was taken. I don't think he even knew her. It wasn't like she went home with him or anything. I mean, I saw her leave with some guy five minutes after that was taken."

"And who did Dr. Byrne go home with?"

"Well, it certainly wasn't me, if that's what you're asking. I'm married."

"I'm just trying to understand what sort of person he is."

"He's just like every other guy."

"How so?"

"He likes women. Is that a crime? Sure, he drinks at the same bar as the students, but it isn't that big of a town. There aren't many choices. He isn't the only one."

"He has a bit of a reputation. Do you know anything about that?"

Crystal looked out of the window at nothing going by. She sat with her legs crossed. One foot nervously zipped back and forth like it had a short circuit. "I don't know what you mean."

"Did he ever sleep with his students or TAs?"

The lack of an answer was telling.

Rebecca kept pushing. She asked, "Did he sexually harass you in school?"

"I don't know what you're talking about."

"He was your boss. Did he make you have sex with him?"

"I was an adult. I'm married now. I was just having a beer. I don't know why everyone is making such a big deal of this."

Rebecca smelled blood and asked, "What sort of sex acts did he make you perform? I need to know. Is there a pattern of abuse? You're a victim and there are probably others. You can tell me. Did he make you have sex with him?"

Crystal didn't say a thing. She just kept looking out the window.

"You need to come forward. I'm sure there are others. Do you plan to sue? If you were to tell me your story, it would help get people on your side. That way you could get all the money you deserve. Just tell me. What did he make you do?"

"I have to go. My husband will be coming home from work."

"Does he know about the abuse? Is that why you don't want to talk?"

Crystal grabbed her purse and left.

Rebecca had been here before. The seed was planted. After a night's sleep, she was sure Crystal would be ready to tell her story.

Chapter Thirty

Just the concept of a road trip made Arthur feel better. It reminded him of the days before he knew what he wanted in life. Arthur had only the vaguest recollection of what that had been, but he had found it for a while.

The day he had accepted the teaching job was still clear in his mind. It had been a declaration to the world that he was giving up. Arthur had always imagined that the world cared, but that was his ego talking. Nobody cared.

The miles flew by, and he desperately wished he could cruise all the way back to before hope had been lost. The more he tried to remember what happiness looked like, the worse his melancholy became until he finally had to admit he couldn't put it into words.

Arthur could remember one thing: her eyes. They were dark and seemed to have hidden behind them all the secrets of the world. It was those piercing looks that drove him crazy with love...or was it lust? He could remember the sex, but why had so little else remained behind? Was it all the years of drinking? Probably, but maybe there was a clue in the loss.

When he was with her and those stunning eyes, he was drunk with satisfaction as if everyone around were looking at her with him and thinking "What the fuck?" Could that have been it? Was it merely the reflection of himself through her that had passed itself off as love? It seemed disappointingly possible.

Arthur pulled into a truck stop and filled the tank with gas. Beef jerky seemed like the proper snack for a road trip, so he grabbed some and a Pepsi. The TR3 was running like a top.

As he pulled back onto the interstate, Arthur set out to remember facts. Anything he could nail down from the past would do. The radio helped when Gordon Lightfoot started to sing. Arthur sang along. It always choked him up a little.

February 28, 1983 was a fact he remembered. It was the day the last episode of M.A.S.H aired. He remembered it because he decided he couldn't watch the episode a few minutes before the show came on. Arthur had seen the last episode many times since, but on that day he wasn't ready for the show to be over. He remembered when Radar came into the operating room to announce that the chopper carrying Lt. Colonel Henry Blake had been shot down, spun into the sea...there were no survivors.

That was some good writing and a great memory, but did it count? How many times had he seen those episodes in the thirty years since the show went off the air? Still, it was a part of his life, a show that a generation shared with universal understanding.

He recalled the smell of the bakery he had taken her to on their first date but not the name of the place. It was two blocks from where they lived. He could see the interior, the glass case filled with pastry, and the clock on the wall behind the register, but the name was lost to him.

There was the time they went to State College to visit a friend of hers. Her name was a mystery, too, but Arthur clearly remembered a game of pool. The women had been going on about something ridiculous, and he had snuck away to shoot some stick. After three games, he started to piss off the locals. They didn't care for losing.

The fourth rack was set. Her friend was ready to leave, so he promised it would be the last game. The break put the five ball in the side pocket, so Arthur was solids, but he didn't have a clear shot next.

His opponent, some frat boy, made five balls before he missed. The table was wide open. Ball by ball, Arthur cleared them until he was down to one more before the eight. It was a tough-cut shot, but he ran the ball all the way up the rail and in. The problem was the eight ball was now on the other side of the fourteen. There wasn't enough space for a masse, so it looked like he would have a tough time even hitting it.

If he missed, it would be ball in hand. He would be toast. The memory was clear as a cliché about clear things, he knew he might be able to hit the eight if he ran the cue ball around three rails. He said, with a practiced nonchalance, "eight ball, corner pocket, three rails."

He always called his shots as a matter of fact because it looked better if the ball happened to go in. At least a dozen people watched as the white ball zipped around the table, kissed off the eight, and sent it slowly into the corner pocket for the win.

She had been impressed.

For another two hundred miles he tried to piece together their history outside the bedroom. The gaps were depressing if not telling. Eventually, it just made him tired.

Arthur pulled off the interstate and found a motel of questionable quality.

It was a small town in the middle of nowhere. They had a grocery store that was within walking distance of the motel. It was cool outside, and the walk helped work the hours of driving out of his legs. He bought a spiral notebook and a bag of powdered donuts.

When he got back to the room, he called information and got the number. The phone rang twice.

"Hello?"

"Laurie, it's me, Arthur."

"Arthur Byrne, the author?"

He had expected something different. Shock maybe, perhaps anger, or even getting hung up on. He wasn't prepared for casual and timeless. "I used to be. How have you been?"

"I've been doing fine, but I have had to find someone else to read. My favorite author has been slacking the last decade or so."

"I'm going to be in town the next few days. You think we could grab a cup of coffee?"

"Sure, how about I meet you at Wood's Bakery at say noon day after tomorrow?"

"Sounds great. See you then."

Arthur set the phone on the nightstand and said, "Wood's Bakery. Of course she would remember." It made him smile.

Chapter Thirty-One

The room had been a disappointment. Sleep was twice thwarted by a rather amorous couple in the room next to Arthur. When the sun came up, he decided it was time to leave. A diner on the way out of town with its shiny metal walls and fifties music was exactly what he needed.

The waitress was a little more bubbly than he would have liked, but she took his order and kept his coffee filled, so he couldn't complain. Arthur's first call was to Wen.

"Arthur, I tried calling last night, but your phone was off."

"Yes, I hit the road after you left. I turned it off."

"What?"

"Biggus Road Trippus, from the Latin, which means I'm driving to New York to bury some ghosts."

"I'm not sure you can bury ghosts. Aren't they all vapor and floaty stuff?"

"That is an excellent observation. I guess I'm just going to visit some old friends after far too long."

"When will you be back?"

"Before the grand inquisition."

"The feminists are building up quite the little army."

"What about the news vans? Have they left?"

"I don't know. I haven't been back to your place. I'll try to drive by this morning and see if they're still hovering out front."

"I'd appreciate it."

"There is some good news - Kurt and Lawrence have been getting a lot of inquisitive tweets from students who seem concerned."

"I haven't been checking Twitter."

"It's probably best if you stay off social media for now."

"Do nothing. Okay, I've got that shot in my bag."

Wen giggled and said, "That was much better than the burying ghost thing."

"I should stick to sports."

"I've got to get going. Lots to do before class. I don't want to sound clingy or anything, but if you have time to call me when you get to New York, I'd appreciate it."

"I think I can swing a call. Talk to you later."

The bacon, egg, and cheese sandwich was delicious. Morning was normally the time of day he would start to

think of something to complain about, but Arthur decided to take a day off from surly. He was in the middle of
nowhere, so he figured nobody would find out.

If he did the math right, he would be trying to find a
parking spot in Manhattan around noon. Arthur never
had a car when he lived in the Big Apple because he hated parking. As he drove along, it seemed like the perfect
thing to stress out over, but he decided luck was on his
side.

He wondered if deciding to be positive was all it took.
He could make a list as long as his arm of all the happy,
cheery people he wished would die a horrible death. Perhaps they just chose to be happy? It seemed like a plausible theory. He might try it for the rest of the day, or he
might get pissed off at the next stupid driver who cut him
off and get back into his comfortable blanket of angst.

When he finally arrived, he got a room at the Hilton
and paid for parking. It was a king's ransom, but Arthur
was sure it was a sound waste of money. He got settled
in his room, let Wen know he had arrived in one piece,
and called his old buddy Robert Goldberg. He was always
good for a laugh.

Ten minutes of talking with Robert had indeed been
full of chuckles. They made plans to meet for a drink.

Arthur took a shower. It was nice to wash the grime of
travel away. He soaked for thirty minutes. When he got

out, Arthur had an idea about his new novel and jotted down some notes for later.

Arthur had plenty of time before Robert would be at the bar, so he decided he wouldn't bother with a cab. He had an app he hadn't tried yet. He punched the address "121 W 28th St, New York, NY" into Maps, and a little red pin plopped down on a graphic of Manhattan. It read Hilton Garden Inn, which amazed him a little.

As soon as he set foot on W. 28th Street, he felt at home. It was a sunny day. Across from the shiny metal facade of the hotel was Holiday Orchids. A young man was watering the row of potted trees lining the sidewalk, and the curb was wet. It was a tiny jungle right in the middle of the city. Arthur crossed and turned left to head towards the bar.

The McDonalds on the corner called his name. Arthur popped in. After an annoying wait, he had himself a double cheeseburger and orange drink. He crossed the Avenue of the Americas. He had always thought it to be a pretentiously named street. It was fitting for Manhattan.

All along the street were white floral delivery vans. He turned right on Broadway, still sipping on the soda. It was funny, he thought, how back at school everyone called it "pop," but, as soon as he was back in New York, he used "soda." The buzz of the city was familiar, comfortable, and inspiring.

It had been a great place to live and write. In a few blocks he was at Madison Square Park. It was one of his favorite parts of the city because of the famous Flatiron building. It always made him think of the rich history of Manhattan. When the building was first built, there was a draft caused by its shape. When women would walk past, they had to fight to keep their skirts down and their modesty intact. The phrase "23 scadoo" came from that era; the local beat cops would tell the guys hanging around to move along.

Arthur made his way through a sea of yellow cabs. The light changed as he was crossing the street, and he was greeted with a honk and a comment he could only assume was profanity in some middle eastern tongue. "Fuck you," he said without missing a beat.

It was good to be home.

He turned left on E 23rd and continued heading for his destination pin on the app. Robert had said he would like the place as it had just the right level of angst for someone like him. He passed a second Starbucks, looked across the street, and saw the brown and gold sign of the "Bull's Head Tavern."

It was dark inside. Arthur was early by fifteen minutes, which meant it would be close to an hour before Robert arrived. His lack of promptness was almost as bad as Arthur's. He ordered a scotch and took out the notebook to do some writing while he waited.

All around were things that reminded him of a life that seemed almost fictional. The attitude had such color; it made characters spring to life. A couple of ladies with big hair sat within earshot. Their conversation, which had little substance, helped him get back in the wordsmithing groove.

The past was back and it still had all its charms.

The first hour with Robert was filled with talk of family, a lengthy discussion of tennis, and how they had each gotten old. Arthur was a fan of the game mostly because of Robert. They had met in college where Robert was a walk-on in tennis. Arthur hadn't had delusions of being able to play professionally, but it kept him in shape and let him date a crazy, hot Czechoslovakian who was on the women's team. Arthur dated several of her friends, who were also disturbingly attractive.

The stories started after that. Each tale was old, worn, and funnier than the one before. They called them the eighty percent. It was a reference to the oft made comment by the wives of the college friends who complained of how they always rehashed the same memories. The good stories, "the eighty percent," were the ones that couldn't be told in their presence in order to protect the guilty.

Arthur said with tears in his eyes, "Stop, I need a break. The llama story always makes me laugh until I've had a world-class ab workout."

"It's one of my favorites, too. Are you still chasing women far too young for you?"

"I've lost a step. I have to settle for the few who chase me."

"You always did need a wingman."

"In the history of wingmen, you were an ace. I remember that tournament you played at in Lakeland Florida. Was that the summer of our sophomore year?"

"I think it was between junior and senior year, but, yeah, it was crazy. If I recall, we were telling people that you were a star on the European tour and were in town giving me some coaching."

Arthur started laughing again and said, "Yeah, you kept adding in details that were hard to deal with."

"Didn't I say you were fluent in Russian, Chinese, and what was the third?"

"First of all, it wasn't Russian; it was Romanian and that blonde with the spectacular tits wouldn't stop until I said something. I had to make up something..."

"You did, and she bought it."

"Yeah, but that wasn't the funny part. You said I was also fluent in Australian, and she didn't get the joke."

"She was the joke."

"Very true and..." Arthur was interrupted by his phone. "Hey, Wen, what's up?"

"It's really bad. Things have gotten worse."

"Just a second; let me go outside. I can't hear you," Arthur said, holding up a finger to let Robert know he would be right back. He went outside. The darkness was a surprise. "Okay, I can hear you now."

"This woman called and asked if I had ever been pressured into having inappropriate relations with you."

"I can think of several things that were inappropriate. Who knew you were so bendy?"

"This is serious."

"Okay, sorry. What did you say?"

"Nothing at first. Well, I said 'no comment' but that sounded like there was something to hide. I tried to explain that I found the whole line of questioning absurd. She told me that a former TA of yours had come forward with a complaint that you took advantage of her."

"Who?"

"She didn't say, but I got the impression it might have been that woman with Cheryl in the picture."

"That's ridiculous. If anything, Crystal took advantage of me. She was a little..."

"I don't want to hear the details."

"Sorry, go on."

"Anyway, this reporter started comparing you to Jerry Sandusky and making all sorts of accusations."

Arthur didn't say anything. His little problem just got a lot bigger. "Are the vultures still circling about the house?"

"There were thirty of them today. There are rumors you've fled the country. It has gotten out of hand. When are you coming back?"

"Maybe I shouldn't."

Wen was quiet for a bit and said, "You're not serious, are you?"

"Don't worry. I was just kidding. I miss you, too."

Her voice changed back from sad to chipper. She said, "I'm glad because there are still a few inappropriate things I haven't shown you."

"You little minx. Okay, I've got to get back to my friend. I'm having lunch with someone tomorrow then I'll get on the road."

"Good. I'll see you in a couple of days. Stay out of trouble."

"I'll do my best."

Chapter Thirty-Two

Arthur stood as she walked to the table. He said, "You look great, Laurie. How did you avoid aging?"

Laurie kissed him on the cheek and said, "I got a waiver from aging."

"You always had connections."

"What have you been up to?"

"I teach literature, or, more aptly, I mock the uninformed and misguided opinions of painfully optimistic youth who hope to find a life in words and thus avoid getting a real job."

"I pity them."

"You should. I take such pleasure in crushing their dreams. How about you? Since you've not been spending any time aging, what have you done with yourself?"

"After we broke up I went back to school."

"In what?"

"Graphic design. I decided to stop drawing to relax and see if I had what it took to be an artist for real."

"And did you?"

"I've been working for a small company for the last six years. I do environmental design."

"Ads for green companies and stuff like that?"

"No, it's where one designs the sign and art for an entire environment. For instance, I did all the signage for an off-Broadway theater. Of course, the fun part is doing the marquee, but I also had to do the signs that say things like 'no smoking' or 'ladies.' It is fun."

"I'm glad."

Before the conversation could make it to that first awkward pause the waitress showed up to take their orders. Arthur ordered a steak sandwich. Laurie spent some time not being able to decide. She ended up going with the Chef's salad, which is what she always ordered.

"You really went out on a limb with that one."

Laurie laughed. "I always think I'm going to get daring, but it is just so yummy."

"I guess that's how you've kept father time at bay."

"You might be right."

The silence came. Arthur didn't mind. She ate a breadstick, and he sipped his water. The waitress brought their food.

Laure said, "I was watching TV the other day and thought of you."

"Oh?"

"Yes, Barefoot in the Park came on."

"How many times did you make me watch that movie?"

"You liked it."

"Robert Redford and Jane Fonda were hard not to like."

"'Six days does not a week make.'"

Arthur smiled. "That was my favorite line."

"I know."

"I don't see a wedding ring."

"Nope, it turns out I wasn't the marrying type."

"What about kids?"

"I never got around to those either."

"You didn't? But I thought you liked kids and wanted to have a dozen or so."

"I liked the idea of kids, but the reality of them was less appealing."

"Then why did we break up?"

"You think I dumped you because of the fight about kids?"

"Didn't you?"

"No, it was just a good excuse. We were done long before that."

"We were?"

"Oh, Arthur, you poor, dear man. Yes, I'd grown tired of your...well...youness."

"My youness?"

"The whole celebrity author thing had gone to your head. You became unbearable."

Arthur thought about it and said, "Okay, I'll concede that point."

"It didn't mean I didn't love you; I just didn't like you much anymore."

"I can hardly say I blamed you. I didn't like me much, either."

"How about now?"

"I've recently found a few things about myself that aren't so objectionable."

"It took you long enough," she said with a grin.

"It really did. How's the salad?"

"Delicious."

It had started as a get together with an ex-girlfriend and ended as lunch with an old friend.

The memories weren't lost. As he drove east, Arthur replayed the good times in his mind. He waxed nostalgic for an hour. After that, it was time to think about his job. He wanted to save it more than ever.

Chapter Thirty-Three

Normally, he would have begun a long drive early in the morning. Starting after lunch as he had made the road seem longer somehow. It wasn't pleasant.

The first hundred miles were fine. The sky was clear, and Arthur let himself think about the first half of the semester. It seemed as if he had awoken from a long dream...or was it a nightmare? He couldn't be sure, but looking forward to a new day was something unfamiliar and precious.

He thought about Wen and how she had bullied him into the twenty-first century. Arthur couldn't remember the exact moment he switched from curmudgeonly troglodyte to computer nerd, but it didn't matter. He liked it.

He saw rain for the second hundred miles. Arthur had driven into a storm. Now the windshield wipers were doing their best to lull him to sleep. He drank his Pepsi to stay awake. You have to keep going, he thought.

It didn't work. Arthur tried the radio. He knew that if he could make it through the weight of sleepiness he would be fine. Still, it was like a great wave was pulling him under.

He had been through this stage on other long trips. He always had the desire to get where he was going. When it got too bad, he would sleep in a rest stop and continue after an hour or two. This time he refused.

The song, "Crocodile Rock," came on, and he tried to sing along. He shook his head from side to side, but the wipers still tried to knock him out. "Fuck! Wake up!"

Arthur started to think about Hemingway. He hated his writing, but The Old Man and the Sea leapt into his consciousness. It was the least objectionable of all Ernest's writings.

Arthur checked the speedometer. It was a steady sixty-five. He realized the limit was seventy and sped up. A semi with a giant loaf of bread painted on the trailer passed him.

Arthur got in behind the truck and let it run interference. All he had to do was stay behind him, and he would be fine.

The thoughts danced about in his head, moving too quickly for him to make sense of them all. He wished he had a slice of dolphin to chew on. That would replenish him. Arthur said, "Goddamn it. You're using references to 'Old Man' to try to clear your mind. Fuck!"

A sign said there was a truck stop in thirty-two miles.

He could make it that far with the help of the giant loaf of bread. He would get a sandwich, another Pepsi or maybe a Diet Mountain Dew, and some chips. That would put him right as rain.

It wasn't the sort of thing he would normally say as the phrase never made much sense. Robert Barr had used it in his book In the Midst of Alarms, 1894. The downpour had gotten to him.

"Clear your head, damn it. Only..." Arthur looked for the next mile marker. When he saw it, he said, "Fuck, thirty-one miles to go."

He thought about the time Robert and he visited a friend at the University of Northern Iowa. It was a long drive home, too. They spent the day drinking, and she begged them to sleep on her floor. Youth and bravado wouldn't allow it.

They promised to take turns, but, three miles outside of Cedar Falls, Robert was snoring. Arthur did fine for the next hour but started to fade. He punched Robert in the arm and told him to get up. Robert did for about five minutes before he was out again.

It had been the same sort of terrible sleepiness that wrapped around him now. The reason Arthur believed he could fight through it came from that night. The blue

208

clock on the digital radio had gone from 3:59 to 4:00, and the voice in Arthur's head had panicked.

He started to yell, "Rob, get up! It's four o'clock. The cows will be on the road." The terror in his voice had done the trick. His best buddy woke up.

"What happened?"

"It's four o'clock. The cows will be out on the road. I don't want to hit them. I love cows. You need to help me."

The absurdity of Arthur's delusion didn't register with Robert. It seemed reasonable. He said, "Shit, you're right. Slow down and turn on your high beams. You want me to drive?"

"No, I got it. You just keep an eye out for them."

The madness went on for an hour. Eventually, he pulled over to let Robert drive. The buzz from the beer started to wear off, and Robert started to giggle as they sat on the side of the road. It was as if some giant cosmic joke had been played on the two of them, and they both got it at the same time. At that moment, neither one was tired. They enjoyed the rest of the trip.

Arthur just needed to make it past the cows.

He rubbed his hand over his face and rolled down the window. The spray from the rain helped a little, but it was cold, so he rolled the window back up.

He couldn't lose the loaf of bread and panicked a bit when a VW Bug got between him and the truck. A moment later the car pulled back into the fast lane. Arthur bid it good riddance. He saw he had seventeen miles to go.

What was his great fish? Was it Mary? No, though he did spend a mile thinking about lashing her to the side of his TR3 and having land sharks eat away at her underbelly. It would be a less sad ending than what Ernest had come up with.

No, it wasn't Mary.

Was it his job? That didn't sound quite right, either. The book wasn't about fishing; it was about life and never giving up. What was Arthur chasing?

It might be social media or maybe technology. That wasn't it, but he was proud of how the course had gone thus far. The students seemed to be learning something of value. Arthur got the sense the class had value.

The near perfect attendance had shocked him at first, but he started to get the appeal. Social media was the new world, and he was the ship's captain taking them to a new life of limitless possibilities.

Fourteen miles.

A blue Dodge Ram pick-up passed him. The license plate read "Blue 85." He had no idea what it meant, but the Old Man hooked the fish after eighty-four days of getting blanked. It was his eighty-fifth day at sea, and Arthur couldn't get the damn book out of his head. It was like a bad jingle around the holidays that stayed with him for days.

Brian D. Meeks

The first thing Arthur was going to do when he got home was read some Kafka and cleanse his palette. He tried to compare his plight to that of the cockroach, but it just didn't take.

The list of books he loved was long. Old Man and the Sea wasn't on it. Arthur wished he had gotten Call of the Wild stuck in his brain. Jack London could tell a story.

The fatigue was unbearable. He couldn't do the math exactly, but, at seventy miles per hour, he was only ten minutes out from stopping.

The rain went from hard to punishing. The loaf of bread slowed to forty-five miles per hour. Arthur couldn't see anyone in his rear view mirror. The visibility to the side was almost zero. He was truly lost at sea.

If he could only see the lights of Havana, he would be able to use the favorable trade winds to find his way home. Seven more miles to go...then nine more hours after that.

Chapter Thirty-Four

At 9 p.m. the pizzas arrived. The war room had started twenty-four hours before by Kurt. He and Wen had been talking about the state of things with Dr. Byrne when he got the idea.

He called Lawrence and asked, "What are you doing?"

"Nothing. Just watching TV. What's up?"

"I'm here with Wen. We were thinking of putting out a call for reasonableness."

"What in the world do either of you know about reasonableness?"

"That's why I'm calling," he said laughing.

"Okay, I'll be right over."

Susan and A. were Kurt's next calls.

They each started by writing blog posts defending their favorite professor. A few students saw the posts and got on board with their own opinions. By midnight, the comments were adding up. Everyone seemed encouraged.

They worked Twitter mainly but also StumbleUpon, Digg, and Delicious. Wen even mentioned their "movement" on Foursquare when she went out for coffee at 6 am.

By mid-morning, seven students had joined them and were asking their Facebook friends to "like" the "Save Dr. Byrne" page. The hashtag #Unfair hadn't gathered much traction.

The trolls started to attack with venom typically reserved for politics around noon. The leader of the feminists who were calling for Dr. Byrne's head wrote a rebuttal piece. Her following dwarfed the combined following of the TAs' blogs.

Despite their best efforts, there were far more people who wanted to see justice handed out swiftly and, in many cases, with clubs. Wen kept posting responses that it was a picture of two consenting adults. She was viciously attacked and called a whore.

The Huffington Post jumped on the bandwagon around 8 pm and reposted the piece by the opposition. The Post suggested the hashtag #Firehim. It began trending within ten minutes.

Tired and hungry, they nibbled on the pizza in silence.

Wen began to weep a little. She tried to fight them, but the tears wouldn't obey.

As Kurt put his arm around her, he said, "I think Dr. Byrne would quote Burns, 'The best-laid schemes o' mice an' men gang aft agley.'"

"We've made everything worse."

"Yes, we have. It sucks."

Lawrence said, "I don't understand how people can ignore the facts and go straight to hate."

A. said, "Some people just like tearing others down. It is all they know."

Susan said, "That is so cynical...but probably true. The pizza's good, though."

Lawrence asked, "Why didn't our stuff go viral?"

Kurt answered, "I think it is because the people RTing are all students and their followers are each other. It was a small audience that got on board, and they don't have much reach."

A. said, "It reminds me of the Duke lacrosse scandal."

Wen said, "That went on forever. By the time the woman admitted to lying, it was too late. They were screwed."

Lawrence said, "I should have never thrown that party."

Wen replied, "It was a great party. You're not to blame. It was that stupid article in the paper."

Lawrence gave a shrug and grabbed another piece of pizza.

Arthur parked in the alley just after 3 am. The moment he walked through the back door, Maltese greeted him with a somewhat angry meow.

"I know. I'm sorry I left. Did Eric take good care of you?"

The silent treatment that followed was brutal.

Arthur got the jar of cat treats. Maltese decided it was really no big deal that he had left. All was forgiven.

It seemed like a bad idea to turn on the lights. With only a tiny move of the blinds, he could see people were still living on the street outside. Could it really be such a big story? At that moment, it didn't matter. He needed sleep.

Maltese kept an eye on Arthur. As soon as he was in bed, the cat hopped up and settled onto the pillow.

Shortly after the sun came up, Maltese remembered that Arthur hadn't been around to pay attention to him and decided it might be best to get an early start on making it up to him. It only took two short meows and a really long one to do the trick.

Arthur pulled the cat up on his chest and stroked his fur. The purring was therapeutic, but he knew that it wasn't going to be a great day. He had only one thing on his agenda besides avoiding the pack of jackals outside and that was calling his lawyer.

Maltese seemed satisfied and drifted back to sleep. Arthur was close behind.

The morning consisted of incoming calls from Wen, Lawrence, and Kurt who were all concerned about the state of affairs. Additionally, Arthur's attorney put him on the clock and began his first billable hour. His lawyer had seen The Huffington Post piece and thought he might hear from Arthur.

Arthur skipped breakfast as he didn't have much of an appetite. Maltese ate twice.

The assembled media jackals figured out he was home. Periodically, Arthur liked to move the curtain to get them all worked up. When the doorbell rang, he feared that the fourth estate was storming the castle.

It turned out to be a middle-aged man in khakis and a buttoned down shirt. He didn't appear to have a microphone or camera, so Arthur opened the door but left the chain on. "May I help you?"

"Dr. Arthur Byrne?"

"Yes."

He shoved a large envelope through the opening and said, "Consider yourself served."

"It would be insincere of me to say thanks."

"I understand. Don't sweat it. At least you didn't spit on me."

Arthur closed the door.

He sat in his favorite leather chair. Arthur closed his eyes and did a breathing exercise he learned in college. It didn't help.

Brian D. Meeks

A second call to his attorney was unavoidable.

While they were talking, Eric let himself in and grabbed a seat on the couch. Maltese greeted his substitute human by crawling onto his lap. The ear scratching led to some appreciative purring.

"What was that about?" Eric asked.

"I'm making a down payment on my shyster's place in Boca Raton. He's got me on the clock. Oh, and I'm being sued for sexual harassment by Crystal."

"She was the one from a couple of years ago?"

"Yes, with the big hands."

"Didn't she once show up at three in the morning wearing a French maid's outfit?"

"I had forgotten about that," Arthur said. He got up and grabbed a notebook. "I should probably mention that the next time I'm spending $500.00 an hour on a phone call."

"A new phone sex line?"

"I meant my..."

"I know. I was kidding. What's the next move?"

"I've been told to stay in my bunker and not to speak to the press."

"You need anything?"

"I could use some food. I'm not sure Maltese is willing to share."

"Make me a list and I'll pick it up."

"You're a good man, Charlie Brown."

"I just can't understand how this has become such a big deal. When did having young women fancy you become a crime?"

"Fancy? Really?"

"I've been watching a lot of BBC America lately."

"That explains it then. Now I'm craving fish and chips."

"How was New York?"

"Laurie and I had lunch. You know what?"

"No, what?"

"I've been lamenting a romantic notion that never was."

"That's good."

"It is?"

"No, I mean, you should write that down. It's a nice bit of writing, or it would be if you put it to paper."

Arthur flipped the page on his notebook and asked, "What did I say? I wasn't listening."

"'I've been lamenting a romantic notion that never was.'"

"I do like that."

"It's not the sort of thing that wins a Pulitzer, but it sounds like your old voice. How's the writing going?"

"I've put quite a bit together in my head. The last few hours on the way home I lost myself in the story. I guess I'll have plenty of time to write it down while I'm in the bunker."

Eric eased Maltese off his lap, took the grocery list from Arthur, and headed out.

Arthur didn't see any reason not to do some writing, so that's exactly what he did.

Chapter Thirty-Five

Arthur opened the door to find Kurt standing on the steps with a couple of Subway sandwiches. "Come on in. How are things out there in the wild?"

"It looks like your media contingent has thinned some."

"Yes, the last three days have seen them scurry away. I'm hopeful they've grown bored and that the rest will give up soon."

"Are you getting cabin fever?"

"I'm the Danny Terrio of cabin fever."

"I suspect that is one of your old people references."

"It was a show called Dance Fever. He was on it and also in the movie Saturday Night Fever."

"A double fever reference. Nice, but I don't care."

"What brings you around?"

"I've had an idea."

Brian D. Meeks

Arthur got them a couple of beers, and they chatted as they ate. Arthur had the BMT while Kurt went with the meatball sandwich. Kurt made the "balls" joke before Arthur could get it out. Arthur laughed and raised his beer to toast the quick wit.

After they ate, Kurt got the computer set to go.

"Okay, explain it to me again. Why are we using Skype?" Arthur asked.

"It's the same as a phone. Don't worry about it. You just need to put on the headphones and talk." Kurt said.

"You know the number?"

"Yes, I have it from the history on your phone."

"You're very clever."

"This may not work, you know."

"It's worth a shot."

"Okay, I'm dialing now."

The phone rang. A cautious voice answered, "Hello, this is Crystal."

"What are you doing?"

"Arthur, is that you?"

"Of course it's me. Or are you suing someone else, too?"

"My lawyer said I'm not supposed to talk to you. He warned me you'd probably call."

"It seems he was right. What did I do to piss you off so much?"

"I shouldn't talk about the case."

221

"There isn't any case. You know full well I didn't sexually harass you."

"That reporter got me thinking. I need to go."

"Come on, don't hang up. I just need to understand what's going on. I'm not asking you to drop the suit or anything. What did I do? You know what we had wasn't just some fling."

Kurt smiled and made circular motions with his hands.

Arthur nodded and rolled his eyes as he continued, "I thought we had something special, but you graduated and moved on. Heck, you're the one that got married. What's going on? You owe me that."

"I suppose I do. Okay, I'll tell you, but it has to be off the record."

"I'm not a reporter. I'm the defendant."

"I totally feel terrible about that, but you have to understand my husband was really pissed off about the photo. He didn't know about us."

"You weren't even doing anything in the picture. Why did you tell him about us? You could have made something up. Lying is the cornerstone to any marriage."

There was a long silence.

Crystal said, "I should have lied. I didn't think of it. You know I'm not quick like that."

Arthur held up his hands and affixed an internationally recognized expression of incredulous.

Kurt was trying not to laugh.

She continued, "We had a fight. Then I remembered what that reporter said."

"What reporter?"

"Rebecca. She kept pushing and asking if I had been taken advantage of in college."

"Yes, but if anything, you took advantage of me. I seem to remember you having a collection of handcuffs that would make a secret service agent blush."

Crystal giggled and said, "Yes, I do like my toys."

"Then why bring the suit?"

"I had to tell my husband something."

"In some strange way I guess I see your logic. So you love him, do you?"

The next pause was uncomfortable.

"Yes, I guess."

"Well, you gotta do what you gotta do. I get that. May I ask you one more thing...off the record?"

"Sure."

"You don't really feel like I took advantage of you, do you?"

"No, of course not. I'm really sorry."

"Well, you were special, and I mean that in ways you can't begin to understand. Talk to you later."

"Don't tell anyone about our talk, okay?"

"Dear sweet Crystal, you have a great day," Arthur said.

Kurt hung up the Skype call. "Wow, she is spectacularly stupid."

"Did you get that?"

"Oh, yes, it was all recorded," he said and started laughing.

"What?"

"Off the record?"

"Yeah. I know."

"Should I leak this to the world wide web with a snarky blog post?"

"Not yet, but make a copy and keep it as a back-up."

"You think someone might try to steal it?"

"I'm more worried about me accidentally deleting the file. I'm still frightened by that cyborg thing you and Wen have made me adopt."

Kurt shook his head. "We should send this .wav file to your lawyer."

"Here, let me open my email. I've got his address in there."

After Kurt hit "send," Arthur handed him another beer. "It was a good idea. I owe you one."

"Cheers."

"You mind doing one more thing for me?"

"What's that?"

"Find out what you can about this Rebecca person."

"Will do."

Chapter Thirty-Six

"President Grosvenor, your eleven o'clock has arrived."

"Show her in."

Rebecca, wearing a pinstripe suit and serious glasses, introduced herself and took a seat.

"What may I do for you, Rebecca?"

"You have a professor in the liberal arts department, Dr. Arthur Byrne, who is currently under suspension and awaiting review. Is that correct?"

"The review is being handled by the dean of the department, Mary Shingle, but, yes, I'm aware of the situation."

"What was the reason for his suspension?"

"We have very high standards with regards to the conduct of all our employees, especially members of the faculty."

"What, specifically, was he suspended for?"

"You will need to speak with Ms. Shingle for specifics. I don't speak on her behalf. She has expressed concerns about his behavior after a rather salacious photo of Dr. Byrne was run in the student paper."

"You refer to the photo of him in the bar with a partially naked woman on his lap."

"Again, I'd refer you to Ms. Shingle for more details."

"Are you aware that papers were filed and that Dr. Byrne was served a summons to appear for a deposition in a lawsuit alleging that he sexually harassed a former teaching assistant?"

President Grosvenor paused to consider his words carefully. "It is not the policy of this university to comment on such matters."

"I'm not asking for a comment, only an acknowledgement as to whether you were informed of his situation."

"I'm not at liberty to discuss any ongoing litigation that may involve members of faculty."

"Does Dr. Byrne have a history of taking advantage of his subordinates?"

"In the ten years he has been teaching here, there has not been a single complaint, of that, I am sure. Who is this former employee who has brought the suit?"

"Since you don't know her name, I'll assume you were unaware of the suit before now."

It was a blunder, and he knew it. Grosvenor leaned back and touched his fingertips together. He said nothing further and considered whether he should throw her out of his office.

Rebecca said, "At Penn State, Jerry Sandusky abused children under the noses and with the knowledge of many high-ranking officials within the football program. Have you been covering up a pattern of serial..." she paused for effect and added "...womanizing, possibly bordering on assault?"

"Don't you dare compare Dr. Arthur Byrne with that monster. Sandusky was abusing young people within a sports program. There has never been a single complaint brought by a female member of staff..."

"Until now, you mean. How many years went by before we found out about Sandusky? Who knows how many women have yet to come forward. Rape victims are often afraid to admit what happened to them."

"This interview is done," he said and stood. He glared at the young reporter as he made a gesture to the door.

She closed her notebook with a look of smug satisfaction and said, "I'm sure I can find more victims. People like him never prey on just one woman." She dropped her card on his desk and added, "If you wish to go on the record with anything more, before, you know, to tell your side of the story...and possibly save your job..."

"Please leave before I call security."

When she was gone, he said to his secretary, "Please find Dean Shingle and tell her I need to see her immediately if not sooner."

"Are you all right?"

"I'll be fine. Please find Mary for me."

Grosvenor closed the door and poured himself a drink. He drank it and added two more fingers worth before he sat back down at his desk. He dialed Arthur's number.

"Hello."

"Arthur, Grosvenor here. How is it going?"

"I'm on suspension. How do you think?"

"Yes, things have gotten a bit out of control."

"Was this your doing or did Mary cook up this idea on her own?"

"I'm not sure I like your tone. Are you implying that we had anything to do with this mess? It was your face splashed all over the paper. Why do you insist on cavorting with women half your age?"

"To answer your first question, I was implying exactly that. As for why I might cavort, as you say, with younger women, I say this: because I can. We are consenting adults. I don't fool around with students anymore."

"Arthur, you know I like you, but this has to stop. What is this about a sexual harassment suit?"

"I'm being sued."

"By whom?"

"You remember Crystal. She wore the red dress that showed off her considerable…"

"Yes, I remember her. She wore it to the Christmas party if I recall."

"If I recall, you commented about the cut of the dress twice."

Grosvenor took a long pull from his drink and sighed. He said, "I don't remember making any such comments, but, yes, I do remember her. Is there any merit to this suit?"

"There is not."

"Are you sure?"

"What about this hearing? I may not be a model employee, and I'll admit to a certain disregard for the decorum of academia, but the SMS 301 was going well. I didn't want to teach the stupid thing, but I did. Attendance was at nearly 100 percent."

"So I've heard."

"Then why is Mary on the war path?"

"Why do you care? You've always made it clear you were too good for teaching."

Quiet settled over the call.

"Arthur, are you still there?"

"Yes. I'm just thinking. You're right. I've been an arrogant S.O.B. since day one. I probably owe you an apology, but, since I suspect your fingerprints are on that story, I'm not paying up."

"What's the bottom line?"

"That's what I'd like to know."

"I'm not following."

"I'm being run out of town on a rail, and, for the first time, I think I actually mind."

"I've got to go. I have another call. You're sure the suit doesn't have any merit?"

"I am," Arthur said and hung up.

Jonathan didn't really have another call. He needed to think, and he could only take Arthur in small doses.

Chapter Thirty-Seven

Rebecca was pretty but in a wholly generic way. She had been the head cheerleader in a tiny high school. Her first job, which she considered beneath her, was running a register at the Wal-Mart on the edge of town. Among the blue-clad crew she was a flawless diamond who shone so brightly that one had to look away for fear of permanent retina damage. Despite loathing her job, she considered it a character flaw to not excel. She was employee of the month for an entire year until the manager called her in. He explained that though she was still the top employee, they were giving it to Ellen because her father had passed and the fifty-dollar bonus was much needed.

Rebecca had graciously accepted an end to her reign, though it secretly ate her up inside. She could no longer look at the wall covered in her head shots. It wasn't just any Ellen who had been given her award; it was the same girl who, after the summer between sixth and seven grades, had returned to school with attention-grabbing breasts. It had been an unforgivable transgression.

It wasn't until Rebecca stepped foot on the University of Iowa campus that she encountered the limits to her charm and physical appeal. Iowa City was crawling with women who were pretty, charming, and dead set on getting their advanced Mrs. degree after four years of sorority life.

Serious girls were on campus, too, but she couldn't be bothered with them. Those girls weren't even in the game. After a year of thinking she might get a business degree, she declared a journalism major. She had written some stuff for the high school newspaper, so it seemed like a plausible choice.

A member of the Tri-Delta sorority, Stacy, dated Mark who was a senior in journalism. Rebecca hated everything about Stacy but especially the way she said she came from the "North Side" of Chicago. Stacy had a BMW, fake boobs, and shiny hair that seemed to be unaware of the concept of "bad hair days."

Journalism became Rebecca's passion when Mark was nearby. She subscribed to the New York Times and kept abreast of the important articles and bylines. He read it daily, and she was always ready to chime in on the most current of events and always from the correct point of view.

Rebecca, wearing a plaid skirt and white blouse, just happened to run into Mark at the library. She had some questions about journalism and writing and how he got so many good ideas for his articles in the Daily Iowan. Once he was talking about himself, she fawned until he suggested they go get a drink.

Rebecca never thought of herself as a booty call but when he graduated and left for The L.A. Times with Stacy, who now wore a massive diamond, by his side, Rebecca slid into an abyss of rage that stayed with her to this day. Rebecca was no longer petty and jealous; she was angry. It wasn't just Mark but all cheating bastards like him.

Her journalism degree landed her an internship at a small paper. Though she never slept with any of her bosses, there was an air of eventuality and hope that hung about her, which made an offer of permanent employment a foregone conclusion.

Once she was ensconced, she wormed her way into the best stories. Still, the best stories weren't that interesting. For two years she had been looking for something that would get her noticed outside of Nowheresville, USA.

She hated the small town. Rebecca had long ago set her eyes on New York where she would make a name for herself and laud it over the Marks of the world. This story was the punch on her ticket.

It was late. A few people were still working on stories, but most people had left for the day. Rebecca had turned

233

in her copy earlier in the day, but she wanted to give it a little more polish.

She banged away on her laptop and carefully skirted the edges between facts and reasonable assumptions. Rebecca wove in the questions from her interview with President Grosvenor and, with great flare, used his non-answers as ringing indictments of Arthur.

Somehow, in her mind, she had cast Stacy as the victim during her affair with Mark. It didn't matter that Mark had waited for Stacy and not Rebecca at the end of the wedding aisle; she was the one to be pitied. Crystal reminded her of the girls of Tri-Delta. It was easy to feel sorry for her from Rebecca's lofty and enlightened perch in the fourth estate.

Though she hinted there were others who would come forward, she had found nobody willing to go on record. It was easy to dig up names of women who had been involved with the literature professor but none would say a bad word against him. She wrote, "Of the many women who fell under the professors spell, none were willing to revisit the memories they had long since buried. It is only the bravest among them, Crystal, who has come forward to shed light on his long history of abuse."

Her editor had questioned if it was wise to go so far as to claim abuse. Rebecca, after undoing one button, had stormed into his office, leaned over his desk, and demanded that he trust her. She knew the facts, and they were ironclad. Arthur was a monster. It was their job to stop him. She emphasized the word their. It would run as she had written it.

In the editor's defense, his wife, a beast of a woman, had left him two months earlier because "she wasn't attracted to him anymore." It had left him with a blind spot with regards to Rebecca.

She closed her laptop, satisfied that there was nothing more to be done.

Chapter Thirty-Eight

In one day Arthur would appear before the committee who would judge him, he imagined, harshly.

The reporters had tired and gone home. He was free to leave the house.

The refuge of his tiny home and the slow moving clock had provided ample opportunity to continue with his new story. He wasn't sure where it would end, but the journey had been enjoyable. He liked the characters and their tale.

Arthur missed Wen. They had decided it best that she not come over before the inquisition. Eric visited once or twice, and Kurt came over to help with getting Crystal's confession recorded, but, besides that, it was him and Maltese.

He had had time to read. The books were comforting, but each one was well-used. He wanted something new. The bookstore would help.

A tiny bell let the staff, which consisted of a man in bifocals and grey tabby named Elizabeth Bennet, know that a customer had arrived. Lizzy purred at his leg. Arthur picked her up.

All bookshops should have at least one feline employee, he thought. Arthur carried her as he wandered through the stacks, and she let him. They passed Twain, Turgenev, and Tolstoy, all without comment from his furry helper. Lizzy seemed disinterested in Nabakov, too. Arthur loved his writing, but he already had read most of his work.

The one saving grace he had found in giving up writing to badger students about literature was that it was his job to read. Over the last ten years he had read much that was great and much that was not. He wanted something new but not fresh off the press. He wanted old but new to him.

Lizzy reached out a paw in the C's and batted the spine of a book by Paulo Coelho: The Alchemist. Arthur remembered the book coming to press. It had been an international bestseller. He couldn't remember why he passed it up.

He read the blurbs. An echo of a comment from the past suggested someone might have used the word "phenomenal" to describe the work. It was entirely within the realm of possibilities that the word had led to his dismissal of the work as trivial.

The first few pages, though, were anything but. Arthur was hooked. He returned Lizzy to her box on the front counter, and her assistant rang him up.

It was time for lunch, so Arthur walked to the diner with the blue awning at the end of the block.

The waitress was college age and nice enough looking that Arthur might have lingered in his admiration of her figure, but he didn't. He noted she was pretty, placed his order, a BLT and Pepsi, and cracked open the book.

It began, "The Boy's name was Santiago." Within three pages Arthur liked him. He read on. When the food arrived, he nibbled at the fries because he could do so without taking his eyes off the page.

Eventually, he ate the BLT. It was delicious, but the sandwich's flavor paled in comparison to the story that Coelho had crafted. It had an easiness about it. On more than one occasion Arthur set the book aside. A passage needed to be discussed, but he was alone in the crowded diner.

A young man, sporting Seattle grunge finery, sat next to him. He knew the waitress and called her by name. From his drab olive-green satchel he withdrew a battered copy of The Alchemist.

Santiago had talked of omens as had the people he ran into, and it seemed to be an important theme of the book. Surely, this was a sign. Arthur didn't believe in signs.

Arthur held up his copy and said, "I just started it."

"It's one of my favorite books, dude. I totally devour it every few months. Have you gotten to the part with the old man who sits next to him on the bench?"

"I just have. How did you know?"

"The bookmark."

"You really do know the book."

"Totally."

"What makes it so important to you?"

"It makes me want to wander and wonder."

"Kerouac did that for me a long time ago."

"I've read him, too. Same sort of thing only this one is more so."

"Are you a student?"

"Mechanic. It's my day off, or I'd be covered in grime and have my name on my shirt. The name's Carl."

"Nice to meet you, Carl. I'm Arthur."

"Why are you reading it?"

"I just bought it at the bookstore down the street based on the cat's recommendation."

"I totally know what you mean. Elizabeth Bennet is a well-read cat. She put me onto Elmore Leonard a while back."

Arthur smiled. He wanted to ask how an auto-mechanic got into books or how someone who liked to read got into fixing cars, but Arthur couldn't figure out how to say the words without being offensive.

"You're probably wondering why a grease monkey reads stuff like this."

"Well, yes, but you did say it was to make you wonder and wander."

"You haven't gotten there yet, but I like to think of myself as the alchemist more than Santiago. Or even the Englishman. I used to empathize with Santiago, but it's changed over time somehow. Maybe that is why I keep re-reading it? Each time I learn something new."

"Where does it make you want to wander to?"

"The desert," he said.

Arthur didn't understand because he wasn't that far along in the book, but he suspected it would make sense later. Carl opened his copy and started to read. Arthur finished his sandwich.

There was something about sitting next to this man, a boy really, reading a book that Carl knew so well, and he, the literature professor didn't that told Arthur there was a point to it all.

It was uncomfortable reading next to Carl. He had a sense he might get called on or that a pop-quiz was eminent. Arthur paid his check and left.

The coffee shop up the street put enough distance between him and the young Coelho scholar and engine expert that he could continue reading.

Arthur sat and read. He read until he was done. By the end, he had more questions than answers, but one thing was clear: if he wanted clarity, he needed to get back home and write.

Chapter Thirty-Nine

The deposition was at eleven; the inquisition started at two. Arthur and his lawyer, Jerry Arches, arrived before Crystal and hers. Arthur thought it odd since the meeting was at her lawyer's office.

Jerry said, "This is going to be fun."

Arthur said, "I have to admit after the last article, I'm ready to take my pound of flesh."

Jerry looked at Arthur and squinted. He said, "I may not be a literary scholar, but it didn't work out so well for Shylock."

"Two points for knowing The Merchant of Venice. Do they know I'm paying you by the hour?"

"They do."

The door was held open for Crystal and her husband. The team of three lawyers introduced themselves. A stenographer took her seat, too.

Arthur didn't pay attention to the underlings' names, but Ms. Paula Kingston scared him a bit. He imagined her long, serious nose, thin lips, and eyes could calculate a person's net worth by their shoes.

His shoes needed a polish, but he knew it didn't matter.

"Gentlemen, before we begin this deposition let me take this opportunity to suggest a number that will save us all a lot of time."

"We are open to hearing your offer," Jerry said.

Ms. Kingston tore a piece of paper off her yellow pad, scrawled a number, folded it, and slid the paper across the table.

Jerry looked at the number first then showed it to Arthur.

Arthur said, "A quarter of million seems a little steep." He took the piece of paper and wrote a counter offer.

Ms. Kingston opened it and said, "I don't think ten thousand dollars is going to suffice."

"It's negative ten thousand dollars."

She didn't understand.

Arthur continued, "Of course, in addition to a check for ten thousand dollars, I'll also need you to pay my attorney's incredibly reasonable fees."

"Mr. Byrne, you do not understand the magnitude of trouble you're in. I don't appreciate this joke. It isn't funny."

Arthur said, "In that case, I'm going to need to insist on fifty thousand…plus fees."

Jerry had a smile that would have cost him a fortune in the poker rooms of Atlantic City. Ms. Kingston noticed, and her expression changed. She didn't say anything for a while. Arthur kept his poker face on, but he could tell she was starting to realize she might be drawing dead.

Crystal was dumb, but she had done the math. Her face had lost all its color. Her husband just looked angry.

Ms. Kingston gave a glance towards Crystal and said, "What have you got?"

Jerry opened his briefcase and removed a digital recorder. He also pulled out a transcript. "In the interest of expediency, I've taken the liberty of highlighting the important bit." Jerry flipped to the third page, spun the document around, and slid it to Ms. Kingston.

She read the highlighted part, then the whole thing. Crystal looked like she was going to pass out.

Her husband said, "What is this all about?"

Arthur said, "In Crystal's defense, she did this because she loves you."

The husband looked suspicious.

"Listen, we hooked up three years ago over and over again…I digress. The point is, it was before you two met. She loves you."

The husband said, "We've been dating for four years." Now, he was furious.

Arthur looked at Crystal and said, "Oh, well, in that case, she cheated on you repeatedly, occasionally wearing a little French Maid outfit that's burned into my memory."

Jerry removed a photo taken at a Halloween party from his briefcase.

Crystal said, "Oh, I forgot about that."

Arthur said, "She's got great legs, a spectacular ass, and her...well, I don't need to tell you."

The husband stormed out.

Ms. Kingston said, "Since this trip down memory lane is costing my client by the minute, I'd like to take a moment to consider your original offer."

Jerry said, "You rejected that offer."

"You're not seriously asking for fifty thousand plus expenses?"

"Actually, we have a third, perhaps more palatable offer," Jerry said as he pulled an envelope out and handed it to Ms. Kingston.

Crystal scowled at Arthur and said, "You really fucked me."

"You always did have a problem with ambiguity. Yes, I did, repeatedly, but you're not mad because of the past or what I just said. You're pissed because I didn't take you home two weeks ago. That guy you married is a chump, and you know it. Take the offer and start over. Maybe you can be happy."

Jerry stood. Arthur took the cue. They went to the hall-way to allow Ms. Kingston to consider their new offer.

They stood by the water cooler. Arthur asked, "You think they'll take the deal?"

"I can't imagine they would try to counter."

Five minutes later Ms. Kingston came out and said, "Well played, Jerry. You've got a deal." She shook his hand and Arthur's and said, "You were a little hard on my client. It was probably good for her."

Arthur gave her a grin. Ms. Kingston didn't seem so scary when she took off her game face.

Chapter Forty

President Grosvenor wore the suit his wife had custom made for him in London. The cobalt blue tie gave him a sense of invincibility though his face told a different tale. He could hear the chants from both sides.

Two hours before, at the president's request, the head of campus security had requested help from the town's police chief. Because Grosvenor anticipated a crowd, the hearing had been moved to the main auditorium with a capacity of four hundred. Every seat was taken thirty minutes before they were to begin.

Outside, all the major networks had crews on hand. At least two dozen local outlets from around the state were in the mix, too. It was estimated that at least 3,000 students split about 60 – 40 in favor of putting Arthur's head on a stick. The chanting was great for B-roll, but it grated on Grosvenor's nerves.

Mary was huddled in a corner with her two staff adjudicators who had been selected for their mental acumen and unwavering belief in kissing her butt at all times. All three demonstrated an unwillingness to make eye contact with the president.

Grosvenor cleared his throat with an authority that would have made Churchill proud. Mary excused herself from the others.

"Glad you could make it, Jonathan."

"Is this how you imagined things going?"

"I'll admit it's better than I could have hoped. The article about the lawsuit was a bit of luck. We will be rid of him before you can say lickety-split."

"I would never say that. Are you at all concerned about the reaction from the students?"

"There are more on our side than his."

"Oh really? Have you looked at the "Burn Arthur at the Stake" crowd?"

"What do you mean?"

"They don't look like students. I'm not sure where they came from but it wasn't the dorms."

"It doesn't matter. It will all be over shortly. I think you'll enjoy watching his head roll."

"Someone's head is going to roll today. That I can promise you."

President Grosvenor left Mary to consider the stakes. He took his seat in the front row.

Arthur and Jerry got out of the blue Cadillac Jerry had hired. The media pounced and hurled questions at them as the security forced a path to the stairs. It was slow going.

Robert slipped from out of the crowd, climbed the stairs, and shook Arthur's hand. Jerry reached out to open the door, stopped, and turned around. He raised his hand, and silence fell over the media. The protestors, both for and against, kept yelling.

Jerry said, "As you know, we are here for the hearing regarding Dr. Arthur's Byrne's alleged breaking of the morals clause. I'm confident that the fair and impartial committee will use their considerable intellect to look through the rumor and innuendo to see the truth shining brightly on the other side."

Arthur resisted the urge to roll his eyes at the verbose statement to the press.

Jerry continued, "Of course, you have many questions, and I'm sure there will be even more after the hearing. We intend to address them at that time."

The yelling exploded again, but Jerry didn't take the bait.

The tables were set in an inverted "V" shape. The one on stage right was longer and had a linen on it. Arthur and Jerry were shown to the smaller, uglier table. It had a single microphone while the other table had three and one gavel. At center stage was a lectern.

Arthur surveyed the crowd. All his TAs were sitting together. Wen smiled and gave him a quick double thumbs up. She was adorable. Kurt and Lawrence looked worried. A. was playing with his phone and Susan mouthed "good luck."

The appointed time arrived. Arthur saw Mary peer out at the crowd from back stage. She made everyone wait five more minutes.

The audience was at full murmur when Dr. Weaverson, Mr. Evans, and Mary filed out from behind the curtain. Mary's first expression was surprise when the crowd erupted in both boos and cheers. It was followed by a look of uncertainty but only for a moment.

She took the lectern and said, "If I could have everyone's attention." She waited, but the yelling continued, so she added, "Please, may I have some quiet." There would be no quiet.

Someone yelled, "You're a hag!" There were post-jeer snickers. Arthur smiled.

Dean Mary Shingle raised her voice and said, "We are going to begin, and I need every one to settle down."

When they did, she continued with a prepared and far too lengthy monologue about the history of the school. She wielded the words "quality, honor, and responsibility" as if they were holy relics from the Crusades.

Arthur mentally noted three brilliant retorts that he would save for later. As she blathered on, he considered whether they could be woven into his current novel. It seemed plausible. His mind soon wandered far away from the ridiculousness that was going on before him.

As his mental voyage drew to a close, he noticed President Grosvenor for the first time. He was sitting in the first row but on the same side of the auditorium as their table, so Arthur hadn't seen him. Grosvenor seemed to be tiring of the history lesson.

Mary wound down her introduction and said, "And so it is with heavy heart that I call to order this hearing to discuss Dr. Byrne's future as a member of our faculty."

Silence hung over the auditorium as she walked back to her table. Arthur was surprised. He expected either cheers or jeers, possibly both, that the proceedings were proceeding, but most of the crowd seemed to have lapsed into a coma during her remarks.

Upon sitting and striking her gavel Mary said, "We shall now begin. For the record, Dr. Byrne, will you please introduce the person sitting with you."

Jerry said, "I can introduce myself, thank you. I'm the attorney representing Dr. Byrne in this hearing and all future suits that arise from this point forward."

Mary looked perturbed and shot back, "I addressed Dr. Byrne! You will get your chance, sir."

Arthur said, "This is Jerry. He is my attorney for this hearing and all future suits that arise from this point forward."

A few people chuckled.

A woman had appeared during Mary's opening remarks and now sat at the end of the table taking notes.

Mary said, "Well, then let us begin. We are here because of a lascivious photo of you and a partially naked woman that ran in the school newspaper. You were cavorting with students in a public drinking house…"

Jerry interrupted, "Neither of the women pictured are current students."

Mary shot back, "I'll thank you to wait until it is your turn to speak, sir."

Arthur whispered to Jerry, "Who says 'public drinking house'?" Since he was on stage, his voice carried. Those within earshot laughed.

Mary's face turned red, but she continued, "The photo, on its own, probably warrants no more than a reprimand and a warning. Sadly, the recent revelation that you have been accused of sexual harassment by a former subordinate and that your proclivity for unacceptable behavior is going to be exposed in a court of law and, no doubt, subsequently rehashed on the TV news stations across the country leads me to the conclusion that..."

Arthur said, "Brevity is a lost art?"

The pro-Arthur crowd exploded in cheers. Many of them stood.

Mary banged her gavel repeatedly, which only made them cheer louder.

Arthur stood and gave the internationally recognized double-hand wave that said "take your seat; thanks for the applause; you all rock."

His supporters quieted.

Mary started as soon as it got quiet but couldn't remember where she had left off. She looked at her notes. It was obvious she had written out every word.

Arthur said, "You were about to say I should be dismissed?"

Mary blushed and said, "Yes, but..."

Arthur asked, "I'm to be given a chance to make a statement on my behalf according to the by-laws, correct?"

"Yes, that is correct. You may proceed Dr. Byrne. Then we will give our ruling."

Arthur waved off the smattering of boos. The anti-Arthur crowd seemed to be saving themselves for the verdict. "Neither woman pictured was a current student. I believe both of them are here today. Would you stand?"

Cheryl and Crystal stood.

Arthur said, "Please state for the record. Are either of you students?"

They both said, "No."

Arthur continued, "Cheryl, in the aforementioned picture that ran in the student paper, you are sitting on my lap, and your blouse seems to have opted out of the photo shoot. Could you explain the events leading to that image being taken?"

Cheryl said, "I had been drinking...a lot."

The crowd laughed and someone yelled, "Show us your tits."

Mary looked up and banged the gavel so hard that it broke.

Cheryl said, "Maybe later. Anyway, before the photo was taken I was standing next to the table pictured. Dr. Byrne and I were having a conversation about music. Some guy grabbed my butt. I turned around and slapped him. His girlfriend threw beer at me, and it soaked my blouse. Dr. Byrne stepped in and stopped me from kicking her ass."

More cheers.

Cheryl continued, "So, while he was standing between us, I took off my shirt, which was see-through after it was soaked anyway, and I threw it in the skank's face. It continued to escalate, but Dr. Byrne calmed every one down, and the fight was avoided. After he sat down, I yelled something about him being my hero and threw myself on his lap and gave him a kiss. It was all quite innocent, well except for me wanting to kill that…"

Mary said, "Yes, that will be quite enough. Thank you, miss, you may sit down."

Arthur asked, "Can the committee see where it was all just a terrible misunderstanding?"

Mary sat motionless while Dr. Weaverson and Mr. Evans nodded. Arthur guessed that Evans and Weaverson were hoping the witness might show everyone her tits…in the interest of justice, of course.

Arthur said, "The alleged…you forgot to use that word on the record, if I recall…"

Jerry nodded and said, "Yes, she did. It was somewhat inflammatory the way she described it."

Arthur continued, "The alleged sexual harassment case doesn't exist." Arthur looked at Crystal and gave a nod.

Crystal stood and said, "I'm the woman who was sitting next to Arthur in the picture, and it was I who filed the suit, but I've since withdrawn it. He never harassed me. That reporter," she said pointing to Rebecca who was in the third row just behind President Grosvenor, "kept badgering me to do it. I never wanted to, and I knew it was a lie, but she said I would get lots of money."

The woman taking notes was writing furiously. Her pencil could be heard scrawling on the pad. Not a soul moved.

Crystal said, "I'm sorry. I apologized to Arthur, er, Dr. Byrne, this morning. There isn't any lawsuit, and there never should have been."

Lawrence yelled, "Free Dr. Byrne!" It turned into a chant. The feminists shook their collective heads in disgust and started to file out.

Mary reached for her gavel, but the head had rolled off the table, and she had nothing to pound. Arthur's fans were now on their feet chanting. Though Mary tried to talk over them, it just didn't matter.

President Grosvenor crossed the stage and stood before the lectern. He said nothing. The chanters sensed they were about to get their victory and fell silent.

Grosvenor said, "It is clear that the suspension was a terrible overreaction. I would like to offer you an apology on Dean Shingle's behalf." He looked down, bent over, picked up the head of the gavel and said, "This review is over. Dr. Byrne, you are reinstated."

The TA's began to clap and cheer and everyone followed suit, except the panel and Rebecca.

President Grosvenor walked to the table where Mary was packing her notes. He shook his head and said, "I'd like to see you in my office on Monday." Before Mary could say anything, he dropped the gavel head back on the floor and walked off stage left.

Arthur looked at Robert who was sitting near the back. Robert gave him a nod and a broad smile.

Arthur yelled, "Who wants to go to Edgar's Pit for shots? I'm buying!"

His students, many of whom were tweeting the results, were more than willing to go to Edgar's. Dr. Byrne's offer was later known as the "Shots Tweeted Round the World."

Chapter Forty-One

Outside the auditorium the media waited for their sound bite.

Arthur let them quiet down and said, "I'm pleased to get this whole misunderstanding sorted out."

One reporter yelled, "Will you be pursuing any further legal action?"

Jerry said, "We are considering all of our options but have no further comment on the actions of any media outlets that may have libeled my client."

Another reporter asked, "Do you feel vindicated by today's results?"

Arthur said, "Yes. I'd rather focus on the future than worry about the past...two weeks." He looked at Robert and smiled.

The next volley of questions were ignored.

Robert stepped forward and said, "Today, we are pleased to announce that Arthur Byrne has signed a one-book deal for his new novel."

A one-beat pause was followed by a cacophony of questions. Over the next fifteen minutes Arthur and Robert hinted at the plot, discussed his long absence, and revealed that the advance was in the low seven figure range.

Susan, who had built up a nice following on her blog, was the first to get the story of Arthur's new book deal out. It went viral, and her subscriptions grew by nearly eight thousand over the next few days.

A. started dating Susan. Arthur never did learn his real name or give him any additional letters.

The crowd at Edgar's Pit became a massive social media meeting. Everyone worked their smartphones, laptops, and iPads overtime. People wanted to hear about the new book, which Arthur gladly described in as much detail as he could. Robert had asked that he not give too much away.

Much less binge drinking occurred than one might have imagined. The bar manager gave away hot wings all night long. At least a dozen people wrote blog posts. Arthur declared that they would all be getting extra credit in SM 301.

Arthur sat in the booth where the problems had started. Wen sat next to him, her laptop open, and said, "You need to start answering some of your tweets."

Arthur put his arm around her and said, "What are these tweets you speak of? I'm a wordsmith. I can't be bothered with such trivialities."

Wen elbowed him sharply in the ribs. "It wasn't a request, bub." She swung the computer so that the keyboard was within Arthur's reach. "Here, I've got Tweetdeck up. It is logged onto your account, so go."

"I don't think this social media stuff is going to catch on."

"You may be right, but there are almost three dozen people congratulating you on your new book." She gave him a look that was three parts scary, one part cute as a button, and one dash of pending celibacy.

Arthur shivered a little, ordered a scotch, and typed, "Thanks, I appreciate it. I've been away too long. I hope I can still craft an interesting tale." He hit send.

Wen nodded and gave him a kiss on the cheek. "Keep going."

A young man two tables over yelled, "I got a reply from the famous author Arthur Byrne on Twitter."

Everyone laughed.

Across the bar, in a quiet booth, Emily and Eric were midway through their second pitcher when they stopped kissing long enough to get back together.

Somewhere around midnight Wen let Arthur stop with his correspondence. Lawrence was sober and offered to drive Arthur home. Wen came along, too.

Kurt and his boyfriend were outside the bar smoking. He gave Arthur one last congrats on his triumph.

Wen came out of the bedroom wearing one of Arthur's tee-shirts. "Are you coming to bed?"

Arthur sat at his typewriter staring at a blank piece of paper. Next to him sat the completed manuscript. "You know the irony of all of this?"

She kissed him on the neck and said, "No."

"I was trapped here. Other than playing with Maltese some each day, all there was to do was write. I don't think I've ever been so productive. Even the drive to New York gave me time to figure out the rest of the story."

She rubbed his shoulders and said, "What are you going to put on that blank piece of paper? And why don't you use your computer?"

"I don't use the computer because I like the sound the Underwood makes. As for this white space, it doesn't haunt me like before. What Robert didn't mention is that there is a second, secret book deal."

Wen sort of hugged and wiggled onto his lap. "I can keep a secret."

"You promise."

"Cross my heart."

"Well, I've always wanted to know if I could do it again."

"What?"

"Write a book that people would buy."

"Didn't you just do that?"

"Yes and no. The book will sell because of all the attention I've gotten. There will be people who liked the last one and some new folks, but what I want to know is if I can sell a book as someone nobody has heard of."

"I don't understand."

"The secret book deal is for a manuscript under a pseudonym."

"What a fun idea. I'm sure it will be great."

"I'm going to need to do all the marketing, probably use that social media stuff all the kids are talking about, and do it anonymously. I might need some help."

Wen said, "I could help!"

"I was hoping you'd say that. In fact, I'd like to hire you full-time as my manager/social media consultant. You would have to list me and the pseudonym as different clients, but we can figure that out later when you're not so mostly naked."

Wen gave Arthur the softest kiss he had ever known and said, "I'm not cheap, but you can afford me. Do you know what it is called yet?"

Arthur was losing interest in talking about writing and said, "What?"

"Does the secret book have a title?"

"It does."

"Well?!"

"Give me my tee-shirt back and I'll tell you."

Wen smiled wryly, pulled the shirt over her head, and wrapped it around his neck.

Arthur whispered, "Killing Hemingway."

They stopped talking about books.

The End

Dear Reader,

Thanks so much for giving Underwood, Scotch, and Wry a try. I hope you enjoyed my snarky look at Social Media.

If you'd like to know when my future novels come out please subscribe to my newsletter. I won't sell your names or send too many notices to your inbox. I reserve it for announcements regarding my new novel releases.

Http://extremelyaverage.com/newsletter/

Sincerely,

Brian D. Meeks

The author can be found at his blog, ExtremelyAverage. com or on Twitter @ExtremelyAvg. His bio on Twitter sums him up well. "I have delusions of novelist, am obsessed with my blog, college football, and occasionally random acts of napping. I also Mock! Will follow cats & guinea pigs.

Reach the Author at:
Facebook Underwood, Scotch, and Wry, page:
Blog: http://ExtremelyAverage.com
Twitter: http://twitter.com/#!/ExtremelyAvg
Email: EcoandleRiel@gmail.com
G+: https://plus.google.com/116061117763797622731/about
Facebook: https://www.facebook.com/Brian.D.Meeks

More Novels by Brian D. Meeks:
- ☒ Henry Wood Detective Agency
- ☒ Henry Wood: Time & Again
- ☒ Henry Wood: Perception
- ☒ Henry Wood: Edge of Understanding
- ☒ A Touch To Die For
- ☒ Secret Doors: The Challenge
- ☒ Killing Hemingway